AF260574

Cock-Eyed Optimists: Gay Romance Erotica
Copyright©2013 Barry Lowe
ISBN 978-1-909934-01-6
Cover art and design by Dawné Dominique

Published by
Lydian Press 2013
Find us on the World Wide Web at
www.lydianpress.com

Cock-Eyed Optimists
Gay Romance Erotica

Barry Lowe

Lydian Press

Contents

All the above titles were originally published as individual eBooks by loveyoudivine Alterotica.

Love is just around the corner…

A Red Rose Before Crying

I was getting progressively angrier as the morning went on. "Denise, I'm okay. There's no need for any intervention. Yes, I will be there, I've told just about everyone. Now, leave me alone. I'm late for work and I have the maintenance guy here to fix up my hot water."

The day started badly when I went to hop in the shower only to discover no hot water. I was fortunate that the building maintenance guy, Trig or Rig or Stig – something like that – was available immediately. I could hear him clanging away at the building's ancient pipes.

Denise's next question had me whispering a reply. "Yes, the blond one. You've seen him around the building. Cute? I've never noticed. Is he?"

I could see whatever his name was in my shower wielding his wrench from where I stood in the living room. I'd never looked at him from the point of view of trade.

"I am not a snob. He's straight. And married."

I had no idea whether either statement was true. I simply wasn't interested in the 'help.' Yes, Denise pegged me correctly. I am a snob. Why should I waste my time with someone uneducated who doesn't have the same interests as me? I don't want a relationship in which I go off to the opera while my boyfriend goes boot scooting. Those sorts of differences do not a satisfying relationship make.

It wasn't the first time someone had flung that accusation at me. Jesse, the great love of my life had also…

The silence had dragged on for so long I realized Denise must be waiting at the other end of the phone for a reply. I'd been daydreaming and missed the question.

"What was it you asked?"

"I know it's a sore point, Ryan," she said. "Especially with Valentine's Day coming up, but it does no good to wallow."

I was pissed off. "Wallow? Excuse me for living—"

Denise wasn't going to let me get away with it. "You call what you're doing at the moment living? Ryan, Jesse wouldn't want you to shut yourself away like this."

I snapped. "How the fuck would you know what Jesse would want?" I'd had enough. "I'm going now. I'll call you later."

I disconnected the phone as Stig/Trig/Prig sauntered down the hallway slopping dirty water all over the floor. I don't suppose he could help it as he was soaked to the skin from repairing the shower.

"Trouble 't mill?" he said, nodding toward the phone.

I felt like telling him to mind his own business but he had been good enough to repair my shower straight away and I didn't want to antagonize him in case I needed favors in the future, so I replied pointedly, "Just friends who want to stick their nose into my business."

"Whoa," he said putting his hands up in mock surrender. "I'd hate to get you on a really bad day." Before I could reply to that outrageous slur on my rather placid character, he went on, "Showers fixed. Nothing serious. Should work like a breeze now. Any more trouble with it, just yell."

"Thanks…uh…"

He smirked at my discomfort at not knowing his name. Anyone with manners would have jumped right in, he merely watched as I struggled with my embarrassment.

After an inordinate amount of time, I merely added the word "mate" to my thanks. That would have to satisfy him.

"I'd allow the water to—"

"Yeah, thanks very much but I do know how to run a shower. I'll put a little extra in your Christmas bonus this year because you've been such a great help."

My voice dripped with the sort of sarcasm I reserved for the working classes who needed to be put in their place.

He tipped his imaginary cap in response before ridiculing my generosity with, "Much obliged, guvnor." The insolence of him. I'd a good mind to report him to building management. I simply don't understand why a classic building like mine, with I would have thought people of a certain degree of education, couldn't find a maintenance man with the same sort of refinement instead of the arrogant buffoon I was dealing with.

After I'd signed the sheet to say the work had been completed to my satisfaction, I closed the door on him deliberately rudely but his response was a belly laugh that I heard as he walked the entire length of the outside hallway. Rude bastard. He'd be getting no bonus from me this year, that's for certain.

I'd already notified the office I'd be late but I didn't want to be later than necessary. I hurried into the bathroom, turned on the shower taps and once they'd warmed stepped in. Big mistake. Brown rust and other gunk cascaded over my body and in my hair; some even making its way into my mouth. It tasted foul. I spat it out along with a string of curses and I heard Stig/Trig/Prick's laughter again as I quit the shower. It was my own fault. I hadn't allowed him to complete his warning. I giggled at my stupidity and by the time I stepped into the clear water spray from the shower, I was having a good belly laugh.

By the time I got to the office, Denise had just about forgiven me for all but hanging up on her, especially after I told her the story of the rusty shower although I managed to wring my revenge out of it by lying that the cruddy water sprayed on the irritating plumber instead of on me.

Denise leered. "Did you tell him to strip off and that you'd dry his clothes?"

"What is it with you and working class men? They're all rough, uneducated, homophobic and sexist buffoons."

"And hot as lava. Besides, who in this day and age uses a word like 'buffoon'?"

"It's a perfectly serviceable word."

"Only for people who live in the nineteenth century. Or wish they did."

"Manners have deteriorated markedly since Victoria died."

Denise knew me well enough to know I was only partly serious. That's why we were friends. Unfortunately, as soon as the words were out of my mouth, I knew I had given her an opening. "Speaking of which…"

"I don't want to talk about it."

"We aren't really talking about it. I just want you to know that all your friends are here for you. Use us."

"If it becomes necessary, I will." I knew for a fact it wouldn't be necessary. I detest all public displays of emotion. I didn't cry publicly, certainly not in front of any of my friends, when Jesse died and I would not succumb as the anniversary of his death approached.

Concentrating on the positive emotions of our five years together rather than his passing on Valentine's Day of all things helped keep my emotions in check.

Foolishly, I had committed to the good intentions of my friends who wanted to help ease me through the anniversary by taking me out while I preferred to remain at home with my music for companionship. I guess that's what friends are for: to invade one's comfort zone.

I had become very insular in the twelve months since Jesse had wasted away in front of my eyes. I'd been happy for him to come home in those final weeks; home to the apartment we'd set up in the way we wanted to spend the remainder of our lives. We were comfortable, we were in love, we had good taste – no, excellent taste. It came naturally to Jesse, in me it was cultivated. I had to fight hard to overcome my vulgar past which held me back far too often to acknowledge. A series of older lovers had beaten the street and the pub out of me – beaten me literally in one instance – to replace it with the boulevard and the opera house. Truth be known, opera tended to bore me. I really am a Philistine at heart although you will never catch me admitting to it.

If further proof was needed, although the apartment's out-size fridge – oops – refrigerator contains a variety of classic dry white wines in the stratospheric price range, they've always tasted like cold piss to me. Now reds, that's a different matter. Biggest drawback? I'm as happy with a bottle of cheapish red plonk as I am with a bottle costing $300. I can rarely taste the difference between a good cabinet sauvignon and a fuck-me-is-that-the-real-price bottle of the same grape variety.

As Valentine's Day approached it was difficult not to become somewhat maudlin. Jesse and I had spent five good years together and had anticipated another thirty or more. We were financially secure, with our own apartment at a prestigious address even though I was very definitely the junior in the relationship. Jesse was ten years my senior at thirty-four and earned a salary at least ten times more than my comparatively meager wage from Harbor City Financial Planners where I was a member of the investment advisors' department. Along with Denise and many of my closest friends.

They had all been devastated for me when a persistent cough of Jesse's was diagnosed as cancer. We had the usual discussion about fighting it together and all those other things people say to each other as reassurance. I supported him all through the operation and the chemotherapy which the doctors promised would prolong his life. Sadly, though, the treatment didn't prolong anything except perhaps Jesse's agony.

It wasn't until he was hospitalized for the third or fourth time that he admitted his condition was terminal and he had but weeks to live. He wanted to return home as he wished to die in his own bed. Those days were the bleakest of my life. I took time off work to nurse him although it even became too much for me at times. Jesse noticed my distress, begging me to go out to the movies or to visit friends just for a break. To my shame now, I took advantage of such occasions to disappear from the despair that filled our apartment. I came close to breaking down myself and those alone periods gave me the opportunity to recharge my sadly depleted batteries in order that I could remain strong for Jesse.

To my eternal regret, we had one of our rare arguments on that fateful day. I was particularly hurt by the manner in which he spoke to me. Of course, Jesse knew my vulnerabilities, especially my lowly birth and upbringing and used everything in his arsenal of putdowns to drive me out of our home. "Go out and find yourself a lover, Ryan. Stop moping around at home. At the very least treat yourself to a sauna and a jolly good buggering so I don't have to look at that martyred face of yours any longer."

Knowing it was the pain speaking rather than my Jesse did not make his words any the less harsh. He wounded me and I retaliated by fleeing the apartment. I needed fresh air and sunlight not death and despair. I walked around for hours, visiting parks to soak up the sun and the life around me, glad there was more than just the world of our bedroom. Perhaps I should have shared the care load but I'd selfishly kept Jesse to myself. I see now it was wrong not to share his last weeks with anyone.

Our friends would visit but they wouldn't stay long because I'd shoo them out saying, "Jesse needs his sleep."

Everyone must hope that the doctors for all their medical expertise are wrong in their diagnosis. I didn't believe in miracles or the power of prayer, I was pinning my hopes on erroneous medical methodology until even I could no longer ignore Jesse's deterioration.

His oncologist wanted him back in hospital where he would be more comfortable and have access to better medical care, but Jesse was adamant. I supported his wishes even though it was a burden. I didn't begrudge putting my life on hold in exchange for the small snippets of togetherness we carved out of his illness.

In the end, however, I wasn't with him. That Valentine's Day we had the biggest argument of our lives and, as I said, I fled to the parks dotted around the city. When I returned home later in the afternoon, determined to make the most of what time we had left and to ignore Jesse's taunts in future, my Jesse was gone although he'd left the diseased shell of his body behind.

It was the only time I cried and I believe my tears were not because I hadn't been with him when he died or because I hadn't told him one last time that I loved him, but because he'd left me to fend for myself. He'd always been the stronger partner and now I had been cast adrift like a boat that had snapped its mooring.

I wept until there were no more tears and then I rang his doctor who organized the medical side of things after which I rang Denise knowing that she would take over anything else that had to be done. I was grateful that she propelled me through the inevitable haze of grieving, the grotesque business of burning the body followed by the tedious tributes and then the bitter wrangles over Jesse's estate.

Knowing that his two estranged sisters would be like Tibetan hawks picking over the bones of our relationship, he'd wound our lives so intricately together that to unpick it would mean they'd end up with even less than the token amount he'd left them. He'd taken the time to explain that they deserved nothing because of their homophobic treatment of our relationship which, in his opinion, was better than their own ill-judged marriages. He bequeathed them the token payment merely to remind them what they missed out on.

They huffed and puffed and threatened to blow my house down but in the end they counted their guaranteed eggs against their maybe eggs if they sued. Then settled for what they had. It saved me a tremendous amount of aggravation.

Jesse had been a moderately wealthy man, much more so than he'd led me to believe. His family always believed I'd gone into the relationship because of his cash reserves. They still believe that to this day, but I was never privy to the full extent of his liquidity. Had I known the truth, I'm not sure I would have been comfortable in such an unequal partnership. Jesse understood what made me tick more than I understood myself, which is presumably why he didn't tell me.

It may seem callous but I returned to work not long after all the legal niceties were tied in a ribbon and deposited in a cabinet at my lawyer's office. Friends advised me to take a year off, travel, get a new perspective on life, but I'm not that sort of person. I need the security of a regular schedule and nothing supplied that more than a job five days a week. I left Jesse's investments where they were; he'd been cautious in his speculation which meant there was little movement up or down in his portfolio. I was set for life but I needed to make my own way as well, not only for my own sense of self-worth but because a life of idleness and profligacy, recommended by some of my more hedonistic acquaintances, was not part of my personality.

I'm not normally a morose person but the death of a spouse does wear you down. It's the little daily things that reveal in ghastly clarity that he's no longer there. Small things such as wanting to tell him about a program you both liked on TV, or something amusing you heard at the supermarket, or turning around while making dinner in the kitchen to tell him his favorite author had a new novel in the local bookshop…

The computer was my solace. I'd become so tired of the continual questions about my well-being that it was a relief to chat to people in cyberspace whose first question was not, 'How are you coping?'

Life went on as before, except now I was alone and I spent less time working on my friendships especially after a few well-intentioned, but inevitably misguided, blind dates set up by my well-meaning mates. I was not even remotely ready for a new relationship. Some of the dates were as amusing as they were good-looking which led to a number of pleasurable evenings of intimacy. A number were even repeated on the understanding that nothing serious would come of it.

Thus the year passed. I thought I could celebrate the anniversary by ignoring it. Not gonna happen; my friends were making sure of that. They believed there was strength in numbers and that their love and support would help me pass the hurdle with the least amount of angst. If that was their plan, the day could not have begun any worse than it did.

Valentine's Day tradition meant little to me as I neither sent nor received anonymous cards or small gifts, so while the office was abuzz with secret admirers, I went on with my work. That is until around 10.30 when a delivery of the most beautiful bunch of wildflowers stopped the office. When I ventured out because of the excited buzz that infiltrated even my sluggish brain, I discovered a young female courier clutching the blooms at the front counter, obviously seeking directions to the lucky recipient.

There was something familiar about the arrangement but it wasn't until the young women approached and asked, "Ryan Brodie?" and I'd nodded my head that I realized the flowers were for me. I gave a startled cry which was covered by the round of applause from my office colleagues. "You're a lucky man, someone loves you very much," the courier prattled as I signed her electronic chit.

Before any of the other staff members could descend on me with their inane questions or snide references to secret admirers, I fled to my office and closed the door hoping I would be left alone. I was trembling, anguish flooding from every pore. I should have known better, for a few moments later there was a knock and the door and Denise stuck her head in.

"Come in," I said. "Close the door."

"Who on earth sent you such beautiful flowers?" she asked as she came over to take a closer look at the delivery. "If you don't want him, I'll take him off your hands. Ryan? Whatever is the matter, you look like you've seen a ghost?"

I could scarcely bring myself to speak in case I burst into tears. "That's…that's the exact combination of native plants that Jesse always sent me on Valentine's Day. I always told him it was a waste of money but he insisted I was worth it."

Denise attempted to be reassuring, "That's just a coincidence."

"I would probably agree with you. The combination of flowers could be a fortuitous accident, but the arrangement is identical, the way the package is wrapped; everything is the way Jesse sent me flowers every year for the five years we were together."

"Is there a card? Anything at all to identify who sent them?"

"Not a thing. Only the florist they came from. And, yes, it's the one Jesse always used."

"There's your answer then," she said. "He must have ordered in advance. Maybe even years ahead. You know what a control freak he was."

I sniffed. "I prefer to call it 'organized.' I don't mind admitting, it spooked me."

Denise plucked the florist's card from the bouquet and dialed them on my phone. Lying that she was my secretary, she quizzed the shop on the delivery. They were more than happy to answer her questions after she explained that she merely wished to know if it was a standing order or whether someone called in personally.

Denise put the call on speaker phone. "Oh, I remember that order well," the shop assistant said. "It's quite magnificent, isn't it? Very expensive, too. A young gentleman ordered the flowers. Quite specific on the natives he wanted included and how to arrange them. I must say, we balked at the details at first but when we made up the order we had to admit his way was the best. I remember, too, he did not wish to add a card."

"Did he leave a name?"

"No, he paid cash. The odd thing was he wouldn't leave a contact number in case something went awry with the order and we needed to refund."

Denise asked for a description of the young man but it was no one I recognized. When she'd disconnected the call, Denise looked puzzled.

"Okay'" she said, "I have to ask this. You didn't order them yourself? At a psychological low point or something, and forget?"

I could have been angry that she would ask such a question but I supposed it was valid.

"No, that's something I would remember. You don't suppose someone in our group who knows about the tradition would have sent it thinking it might cheer me up?"

Denise shook her head. "I'll ask, but we pass our ideas around the group first before we do anything that pertains to you."

I was shocked but filed it away for later. I'd have a few questions once this mystery was solved.

"Someone in the office? One of the staff may have seen the delivery in the past and decided to replicate it."

"To what end?" she asked. "Bit expensive as a gesture."

"Unless he or she harbors an unrequited passion for me."

We rapidly ran out of ideas except for the sheer coincidence of the choice of flowers. That, of course, meant we were no closer to the identity of the sender.

"You sure that description doesn't fit anyone you know?"

"I'm sure."

"Of course, it needn't have been the sender himself. He could have been a go-between."

"This is getting much too complicated," I moaned.

"I'll ring round the gang and let you know if I find out anything."

I love puzzles. Crosswords, Sudoku, find the words, the sorts of things you find opposite the comics pages in newspapers. This, however, was one puzzle I didn't like. On a positive note, which I didn't realize until much later in the day, it kept my mind from maudlin dwelling on the bleaker aspects of the anniversary.

By late afternoon, Denise had hit a dead end with all her enquiries.

"It's a puzzlement," she said.

"If it means anything, I guess the person responsible will make themselves known eventually. If it has been sent mischievously, then it's an abject failure."

At the end of the work day, I rushed home to freshen up for the gang's evening out. We were going somewhere new because they felt a visit to old familiar places might trigger painful memories. I didn't care one way or the other really.

When I slid the key into the apartment door lock, I wondered whether their idea wasn't a good one. My stomach lurched at the memory of one year ago today returning to the apartment...I shook my head to dislodge the memory but it wouldn't stay away for long. I showered quickly and then changed into smart casual gear, wondering whether I should stay at a hotel tonight.

I avoided looking at the bed, going so far as to shower in the main bathroom rather than the en suite. I took my change of clothes with me and dressed in the living room. I was grateful when Denise rang to say she was downstairs waiting in her car. I wasn't taking mine, on the assumption that I might get pissed to obliterate the unpleasant memories. As I hopped into her sports car, a pretension she'd indulged with her first annual bonus, I toyed with asking if could I stay at her place for the evening until I realized that would be showing weakness on my part.

The drive was uneventful; we spent the time raking over the identity of what had become known as My Secret Admirer even though neither of us thought he was any such thing. The other members of our group had been equally perplexed when Denise explained the circumstances surrounding my unexpected Valentine's gift.

We were no further progressed in unraveling the mystery when we arrived at the dinner club that was our destination that evening. It was one of those typical concrete and glass structures that looked as if it could be anything from an Ikea-style opera house through to a strip mall bowling alley. A valet took Denise's prized sports car, giving her the once over in case she was someone worth cultivating. When she noticed, she licked her lips and purred, "See something you like because I sure do."

The parking attendant who was a good decade younger, blushed crimson and mumbled what could have been agreement or an apology. Denise would find out later.

Inside, the club was all mirrors and chrome, but not gaudy. The design was warm and welcoming and we relaxed as we were swept along with other patrons toward the auditorium. This was a newish venue which regularly received rave reviews in the gastronomy press as well as the free hip music journals that littered the mall. The venue usually played host to stand-up comedians – I shuddered at the thought – until Denise assured me tonight's entertainment was a bright young male jazz lounge singer in the Harry Connick Jr. mold.

Considering how crowded the venue was, we were seated in amazingly quick time. Denise and I were early and ordered drinks while we waited. She had a spritzer of white wine and soda water while I got stuck into the vodka and bitter lemon. There were large tables for parties of ten and tables for four, right down to intimate tables for two. I wondered if Jesse would have liked the ambience. It was all unrelentingly middle class from the plastic under the table clothes through to the flickering colored candles on every table to the somnambulant mirror ball that cast a despondent laser-like beam onto people's bodies as they danced.

Our table eventually filled up with the remainder of our group at which point we were ready to order. The only other woman in our party brought her husband, which meant the four remaining men, like Denise, were single. They cast many a longing glance at the number of tables at which groups of females giggled without the support of a male escort.

"Please remember that we're here tonight for Ryan and not to get your end in," Denise admonished as the conversation at the far end of our table turned to permissible pick-up lines on Valentine's Day.

"Let them have their fun," I smiled. "It's the one night of the year when everyone should find themselves a lover."

Denise kissed me on the cheek. "That includes you."

The waiter took our food orders after the drinks waiter had piled our table high with pitchers of beer, bottles of chilled white wine and the lone red for me. I would have preferred the sweet oblivion of vodka but I didn't want a hangover so dreadful the next morning that I would spew my guts up even though it was the weekend.

We were all getting a nice buzz on and had just been served our first courses when the maître D' approached our table.

"Excuse me, folks," he said expectantly. His eyes picked out Denise as the organizer behind our party. "We have a young couple who are very much in love and wish to spend Valentine's here tonight but we find we are totally booked out. Except…"

He gave us time to think up various excuses for not wishing strangers to sit at our table.

"You have a table for ten but you are only eight."

Denise didn't even ask for a general consensus. "Of course, they can sit with us. We'd be delighted," she enthused. She's a much more gregarious creature than I am.

The strangers were brought to our table. As they approached a male voice that I recognized said, "Thank you so much for allowing us to share your table, we really appreciate it."

They were behind me at that stage and I wasn't about to swing my head around to confirm my identification of the male of the couple. I groaned inwardly, hoping my suspicion was wrong. Alas, it wasn't.

"Why, Mr. Brodie, fancy you being here tonight. I didn't think your taste in music went as low as jazz. Are you slumming tonight?"

I was unable to take the sort of offence I really wanted to because some of my friends snickered and Denise dug me in the ribs with her elbow and whispered, "Someone has you pegged."

She did have the decency to come to my defense. "We've heard such good things about the venue that we decided to be adventurous. Ryan tagged along to see what all the fuss is about. He has wide musical tastes."

A few eyebrows shot skywards in surprise almost threatening to hit the very high ceiling.

Then Denise asked the one question I hoped to avoid before excusing myself to flee to the men's room.

"You two know each other?" she asked. "Well, aren't you going to introduce us, Ryan?"

He knew I had no idea of his name but the smirk of superiority on his face gave way quickly to sympathy and he jumped in with, "I'm Geoff and this is Suzie."

Geoff? Where the fuck had I got the idea is name was Prig/Stig/Brig?

Suzie clung to him like a leech to a naked leg. I did have to acknowledge, however, they made a beautiful couple. That, of course, meant that I had now taken the time to look over Geoff (still couldn't get used to his name) and admit he scrubbed up rather well. That his maintenance overalls covered a trim, muscular body was a sin. Perhaps snobbery does have its disadvantages if I missed a visual delight like Geoff.

"How do you two know each other?" Denise enquired, whispering a second question to me, "And why haven't I heard about this man god before?"

"I work maintenance in Mr. Brodie's building."

"You're not at work now, Geoff," Denise flirted. "You can call him just plain Ryan like the rest of us."

Geoff waited for me to respond. I didn't really want to break down the barrier between us but it would be ungracious not to comply.

"Call me Ryan."

I noticed the single men at our table found Suzie a succulent morsel while Denise was drooling over Geoff.

"This is the guy who was in your shower when I rang the other day, isn't it?" Denise asked.

I admitted it. "Look, don't bring that up, you might embarrass him."

"Or you."

"Whatever." This night was not turning out at all like I thought it would. Or wanted, for that matter.

Geoff shared my bottle of red wine as we had our entrees and main courses. Desserts were served during the intermission in the show. Suzie's quiet demeanor was transformed by a few beers thrust on her by the men at our table. Geoff watched with amusement as they plied his girlfriend with alcohol although he made no effort to intervene nor did he prevent her from dancing with the men whose hands seemed to wander down across her ass while we waited for the cabaret act timed to begin when everyone had finished their meal.

Geoff asked Denise if she'd care to dance as his girlfriend was obviously having a whale of a time without her boyfriend. Perhaps they'd had a fight. I was no one's keeper; they could work it out amongst themselves. Impatient for the entertainment to begin – and end – so I could go home, my mood was becoming darker. One number seemed to be the length of Geoff's dancing ability and he returned to our table with Denise who was snapped up by one of the available gang members. Geoff sat down beside me. "Hope you don't mind," he said.

I was still puzzled over my black mood so my response was anything but friendly, "I don't own the chairs."

"Are you always so gracious?" he asked.

I laughed despite myself. "I'm sorry. It's just this is a difficult night for me."

I was glad he didn't question me. To short circuit any interrogation, I queried him about his life. I was never good at small talk so my initial foray into personal territory was gauche. Geoff didn't seem to notice or else he was humoring me. He was surprisingly easy to talk to given the disparity in our social circumstances. Perhaps it had to do with the fact he was putting himself through night school in an effort to gain a certificate as an arborist.

"I have a love of nature," he admitted. "Plants and animals, but my real passion is trees. I try to spend every weekend in the bush."

Hmm, I could see where that would lead to conflict in his relationship with Suzie who seemed like a thoroughly modern city girl if her flirtatious behavior was any indication. Geoff glanced over at her from time to time but not nearly often enough to show any concern even when he caught one of my co-workers with his hand on her breast.

I felt a little stab of jealousy every time he looked her way. I really needed to get out more. Here I was getting an erection over the maintenance man for the building in which I lived. Firstly, he was working class regardless of his aspirations to education. Secondly, he was into the bush and all its attendant evils: mosquitoes, flies, snakes, camping. Thirdly, and most importantly, he was straight.

When the entertainment was announced, Geoff remained beside me not relinquishing the seat even when Denise returned. Everyone played a sort of musical chairs moving along a spot, leaving Suzie unprotected between two of the biggest lechers in the company. She shot Geoff a quizzical look to which he nodded. She relaxed and soon one man had his arm along the back of her chair, while another openly held her hand in his on the table.

Bob Teasle was the singer and I had to admit, even to someone whose supposed preference was for opera, that he was very pleasant on the ear as well as on the eye. Perhaps it was the alcohol I'd consumed, perhaps it was the close proximity to Geoff for whom I was definitely developing a crush, or perhaps it was a combination of the two.

During one of the more romantic slow tempo jazz ballads about love, I definitely felt Geoff's foot against mine. Okay, so it was most likely an accident because it was easy to play footsies under these tables as I'd bumped knees with Denise numerous times early on.

At the intermission, I admitted that I wanted the evening to go on much longer.

"Somebody's enjoying themselves," Denise said quite unnecessarily. It was her tone which rankled rather than her words.

Yes, I did feel guilty that I was enjoying myself on the anniversary of the painful death of the only man I'd loved. But life goes on. I was beginning to think that a year was long enough to grieve. I had to kick myself to remind my heart that Geoff was just being friendly.

When the second half of Bob Teasle's set began, after Geoff had spent the entire intermission talking to me, I was well on the way to infatuation. I was vulnerable, I know that now. One doesn't make friends with one's washing machine repair man unless one is in a bad way.

"A penny for your thoughts," he whispered as the lights dimmed for the second half.

Good, keep the clichés coming. That will remind me how far beneath me you are.

It didn't work. He was charming, he was smart, he knew more about music than I would ever know because he wasn't pretending like I was with opera. He had a genuine love of many forms of music and was not embarrassed to admit to liking Dolly Parton as much as he liked Joan Sutherland.

I was amazed at the breadth of his taste and of his knowledge so I needed the little vulgarities and the clichés he dropped into his conversation to remind me he was merely company, albeit very pleasant company and excellent eye candy, for the evening.

It was inevitable that Bob Teasle would sprinkle his performance with jazz standard love songs which merely pointed up my lack at that moment along with the longing for completion that I'd felt over the past twelve months.

After the fourth of fifth love song, I was in serious danger of losing it. The tears were a gnat's breath away when I felt a hand squeeze my knee reassuringly. It's something I might have expected from Denise but she was seated across the table from me and I knew none of the other men around me would indulge in such intimacy. It had to be Geoff.

"It's okay," he whispered. "Let me know if you'd like to leave. We can duck out without anyone knowing."

I was too choked up to ask about his girlfriend and how she'd get home although I had no doubt any of the men at the table would be only too glad of the opportunity to play taxi.

I wasn't prepared to give in to my distress just yet but another two love songs and I was borderline hysterical, just keeping the lid on it.

Geoff must have read me because he placed his hand on my arm, helping me stand. Denise looked over with commiseration but none of the others appeared to notice as we wended our way amongst the tables to the back of the auditorium. Our attempt at payment was waved aside with the explanation that it had all been covered by Denise. I'd reimburse her on Monday.

I must admit if I hadn't been such an emotional mess I may have balked at accepting a lift in Geoff's battered old Ford Sedan that obviously hadn't seen a vacuum cleaner since the invention of the wheel. He had to throw text books and piles of paper into the back in order for me to sit down. I wondered where Suzie sat when she traveled with her boyfriend.

"Aren't you afraid your girlfriend might…um…?" How could I discreetly complete that sentence?

"What girlfriend?"

I was surprised by his cavalier attitude. "Suzie."

"Suzie's not my girlfriend. She's someone I know from night classes. I just brought her along because she loves Teasle. Almost as much as she loves cock."

"But the maître D'…"

"Oh, that line of bullshit about young love? When I noticed you were there and you had a vacancy at your table, I slipped him a few bucks to see if we could…" He shrugged.

"Why?"

"All will be revealed in good time. Just you relax."

I had a million questions but he refused to answer the few tentative attempts I made to ask them. In the end I leaned my head against the back of the seat but when I was awakened outside my apartment building I found I'd been sleeping against Geoff's shoulder.

"I'm so sorry," I said. "Was I there long?"

"Most of the journey."

"I hope it wasn't too unpleasant for you."

"Nah. In fact, I rather enjoyed it."

He leaned over to pat down my hair where it had been mussed against his shoulder. I was still half asleep and almost missed the brief touch. He got out of the car and came around to my door, wrenching it open to allow me out.

"Thank you, young man. That's very gallant."

He held my arm as he guided me to the front door. Without thinking, I handed him my keys so he could unlock the front entrance and see me to the lifts. I thought he'd leave me there but he took me right to the front door of my apartment, inserted the key and opened it. I felt I should invite him in for a coffee for his kindness but I was simply too exhausted. I didn't need to explain, for he said, "Maybe next time."

I was saddened by the fact there would never be a next time.

I thanked him profusely as I closed the door, stripping my clothes off my weary body as I headed for the bedroom. That was strange, there was a light emanating from the bedroom, spilling under the closed door.

"Who's there?" I demanded although I sounded as threatening as cotton candy.

No response.

I armed myself with a carving knife from the kitchen but it was all bravado. I'd have no hope against a determined burglar. I flung open the bedroom door hoping surprise was my best option but I'd used such force that the door slammed against the wall and rebounded in my face. The only thing that prevented my nose from being broken was the carving knife I held out in front of me. It penetrated the wooden door stopping it inches from my face. I pushed inside but the room was empty, just the way I'd left it, except the light was on.

Then I noticed the bed, a single red rose on the pillow. I swallowed the choked cry that threatened to escape my throat. That was Jesse's surprise every year. He would come home from work at lunch time to leave a single red rose on the bed so I would find it waiting for me.

How? Who?

There was an envelope propped beside the rose. It was addressed to me. My blood ran cold. It was Jesse's handwriting. Someone was playing a really nasty trick. I could scarcely control my hand from shaking as I retrieved the envelope. I made my way to the kitchen to find a sharp knife to open the sealed letter, sniffing the glorious perfume of the single red rose which calmed me down somewhat.

I slid a knife under the flap of the envelope, cutting it neatly, extracting the sheet of paper inside. Before I'd even had a chance to unfold the letter completely I knew it was from Jesse. It was his paper and his handwriting.

I sat nervously wishing I had a drink but too impatient to get up and make myself one.

Dear Ryan, the letter began although Jesse's normally neat, concise hand had been severely limited by the pain and suffering he was experiencing. None the less, it was his.

If you are reading this letter, Ryan, it means you are still grieving over me. I never wanted that. I want you to remember me fondly but I want you to go out and experience life in all its wonderful colors and feelings, especially love. I love you more than any other man I have ever known, that's why I was so cruel just a little while ago. Do you believe in premonitions? I had one today. That I would not live to see tomorrow. I did not want you to watch me die. I suppose human dignity was my last conceit. You will come back and find me gone. So I precipitated a fight. Please forgive the hurtful things I said. I meant none of them. I meant only to spare you. Don't feel guilty that you weren't with me, for we must all go on that last great journey alone. Much as I wished it, I could not take you with me.

I will have a friend with me at the last. He will hold my hand and I'll imagine it's you. He will ease me those last few steps to death. He's a young man, Ryan. A young man you so callously dismiss as beneath us. He heard me sobbing one day when I was wallowing in self-pity and knocked on the door to ensure I was all right. I thought he was an angel. He has taken to visiting me whenever you're not home. He is a good man, I know you'll like him when you get to know him. I know he already likes you. His name is Geoff. Enough matchmaking. I know you are still unattached, otherwise you would not be receiving this letter. Perhaps someone has snapped him up, he is quite a catch.

It's almost time, Ryan. I barely have the strength to write any more. I love you, baby.

The loud sob wracked my body and ripped the heart out of me. The tears would not stop and I moaned so loudly I wanted the world to share my pain. I knew in experiencing it so raw that I was finally letting it go. I could scarcely breathe for the tears and I couldn't see who it was let themselves through the front door and rushed to fold me in his arms.

He kissed my wet cheeks while he rocked me back and forth, allowing me the comfort of tears. I don't know how long I was like this but the front of Geoff's shirt was sopping wet when I finally lifted my head to look into his eyes which looked as red rimmed as mine felt.

"It was you sent those flowers this morning?"

He nodded.

"I'm sorry, Ryan. Jesse's dying wish was that I do this much for him if you were still grieving one year later. He thought that was long enough. He was a good man, Ryan. Just as you're a good man if only you'd let yourself be."

"I don't need a lecture, I need a stiff drink."

"How about a coffee?"

"With a little brandy?"

"Deal."

Geoff knew his way around the apartment confirming that he had once been a regular visitor. He still had the key Jesse gave him which he promised to return when he knew I was all right. His coffee was warm and soothing and we sat at opposite ends of the lounge, our feet intertwined as we swapped stories about Jesse.

Of course, I had more tales than he did but he listened patiently, laughing and even shedding a tear as the story of our love unfolded. I finally ran out of steam, exhausted, worn out.

"I'll put you to bed," he offered and I was too buggered to object.

I ran my hand across his cheeks. I didn't need to say anything and he clasped my hand in his.

As he helped me under the sheets, I asked, "Have you ever thought of calling yourself Geoffrey?"

He laughed. "You are such a snob, Ryan. I'll have to break you of that habit." Leaning down, he kissed me sweetly on the lips.

As he walked toward the bedroom door, I called dreamily, "Geoffrey, please stay the night."

He stopped. Without turning, he replied, "I only answer to the name Geoff."

He was almost out the door before I could bring myself to say it. "Geoff, please stay the night."

He kept his boxers on but I felt the hard cock poking against my ass as he spooned me. Geoff was my connection with the past and might well be my future. I fell asleep hoping.

Too Frocked To Care

It all began as a joke but soon developed into much, much more until it got totally out of control. All because of a misunderstanding that went back years. In the end it affected just about everyone in the gang in a small way although it had major repercussions on my life. On my best mate, Reed, as well.

As kids we were inseparable. We were the same age, grew up in the same neighborhood, our dads worked at the same chemical engineering plant. The group was amorphous, varying in numbers as friendships bloomed or died, people moved in or out of the area, and family loyalties changed. Throughout the constant fluctuations, however, there was one constant: Reed and I were the best of mates. We shared just about everything, from secrets, taste in movies, academic achievement, eating habits, and, in our later teen years, even female sex partners.

We were notorious for a number of years in that if a chick wanted me, she had to take Reed as well. Or vice versa. It was no hardship on the chick apart from having to learn to take two cocks at the same time; both Reed and me are what is commonly called 'hot.' We had no shortage of applicants for a taste of double penetration. It was only much later we realized some of the gang saw our behavior as a bit 'gay.' As a result we took to double dating, and screwing our respective girlfriends in the same room.

There was never any touching between Reed and me although a couple of chicks thought it would be hot to watch us make out. Never. Not ever. Okay, it was inevitable that various parts of our bodies would touch inadvertently and we were both okay with that because we were concentrating on the chick. No way were our sex bits gonna touch though. Nah, not even accidentally. Naturally, we saw each other's bits, but never touched. The closest was if Reed fucked the chick up the ass while I was in her cunt, we could feel each other's pricks through the separating membrane. If I'm honest, the first time it happened, I almost blew my load. The feeling was too hot to handle.

From the startled look on Reed's face he felt something similar. Afterwards, we both developed a real passion for that sort of dp. I never thought about what it all meant until years later. I had plenty of time to think about it when I lost my best mate. Not to a woman, another mate, the army, or any of the countless other alternatives for guys leaving the group – except for that one about losing him to another man which never happened – but of all things, to higher education.

It was sort of expected, almost a tradition that most of us were dumb shits and we'd follow our dads into the factory. It was a guarantee of a job for life. The town, dominated – some would say controlled – by the company that owned the factory, looked after our welfare from cradle to grave. Reed's dad always had a bit of a reputation as a shit stirrer; he was the union rep to the workers for starters. Very unpopular with management, especially when he sprouted the notion that the company needed to get with the times if it wasn't going to get left behind. Everyone thought he was just doing a Chicken Little about the sky falling in.

That is, until the factory laid off staff for the first time ever in its history, blaming it on a downturn in the economy. That was when more people began taking notice of Reed's dad and his predictions by joining the union or encouraging their sons and daughters to look about for something better, more stable.

Reed was a year from graduation when all this happened back in North Karagi, an outer industrial suburb snuggled at the bottom of a valley whose hills corralled a thick pall of pollution belched from the factory stacks. North Karagians escaped to coastal South Karagi on weekends to avoid asthma and other respiratory illnesses, as well as toxic deposits which ate the paint on cars.

South Karagi got pissed off at the sudden influx of their northern neighbors and violence flared, particularly among the youth of both towns. Reed's dad came to the rescue. He banged together civic leaders' heads, north and south, to get them to approve a surf club/community center on the hill overlooking the beach and begged, cajoled and blackmailed businesses in both districts to stump up cash to sponsor the building. He used his formidable powers of persuasion to get the nabobs behind the factory to commit a large portion of the costs.

Then, with a mixture from both locales, we formed the South Karagi Surf Lifesaving Club. There was much discussion about leaving off the South in order to make the name more inclusive but Lifesaving head office insisted the club be named after the beach, so South Karagi the club became. It was one of those ideas that looks good on paper but was never given a chance. Within weeks, the club segregated along north/south lines. The two groups of lifesavers rarely mingled and a system was worked out whereby each district took a turn about on alternate weekends. That's how we settled into an uneasy truce. Surprisingly, it worked.

Reed was often embarrassed by his old man although they were both dreamers, and Reed knew enough that his dad was right in wanting him to get out of North Karagi if he was ever going to have a future. In our final years of high school, Reed put his head down and his ass up when it came to study, no longer available every weekend to party. I had no need of scholastic excellence because my future was mapped out for me in the employ of the factory, right down to my superannuation payout when I turned sixty.

Reed and I often discussed my lack of ambition. He was determined to get out and see the world while I was content – no, content is not the right word, I was 'expected' to follow in my old man's footsteps: small-scale ambition. I'd get a job at the factory and slowly work my way up to foreman; I'd marry a local girl, father a couple of kids who would, in their turn, join the workforce. It never occurred to me to question it. That's where Reed and I differed. He questioned everything, sometimes driving me spare with his arguments which seemed to be merely for the sake of arguing.

"You're too complacent, Thom," he'd say. "The whole town is. The world won't stay like this forever and you'll find yourself lost because you won't know how to adapt to circumstances."

He had quite a line of argument but I didn't want to hear it. "You're just a parrot, mate," I told him once. "You're just sprouting the propaganda you're old man has stuffed into your head." I tapped his forehead hard in an effort to provoke him because he'd been particularly harsh in his criticism of the town and its inhabitants which, of course, meant me and my family.

He sighed without taking the bait. "Have it your way, mate," he said, gripping my fingers but not squeezing or bending them painfully. "I was hoping we could both hop on an express to the future but it looks like I'll be leaving you at the station. If you even bother turning up to see me off."

See, that's what I hated. The way he spoke in metaphor. Gave me the shits. If I'm honest, I was also angry with him because I knew part of what he was saying was true. In the end he was right about me not turning up to see him off when he left for uni after the gang graduated from high school. Vic told me later that Reed waited until the train was pulling out of the station before he hopped on board. I guess he was waiting for me. I wrote later telling him I was with Stacey and lost track of the time. The truth was I was aware of every second counting down to the moment the train was due to leave, harangued into staying away by the self-same Stacey who'd been casting the wildest aspersions on Reed and my friendship. Essentially, it was an ultimatum: her or Reed.

I got an email back from Reed that said, "I understand, mate. We all have to make our own choices."

Frustrating bastard.

I sent him an invitation to the wedding six months later but he didn't reply and didn't show. No congratulations, no wedding gift, just silence. I suppose the news of our nuptials must have come as a bit of a shock because I hadn't bothered keeping in touch about my personal life, not that the whole town didn't know about us, but it was all sort of settled around me. I was a (dis)interested bystander. If Stacey and her parents and friends hadn't recruited my parents none of it would have happened.

Stacey and I had only hooked up once we graduated high school and that was mainly because Reed was leaving and I was at a bit of a loss. The other members of the group all had girlfriends in varying degrees of seriousness, a couple of them headed for the altar as soon as the men began work in the factory and the women could find employment as check-out chicks in the supermarket or apprentices at the multitude of hairdressing salons. Reed told me I could do better and I openly agreed with him, informing him that Stacey was merely a stop-gap measure until someone better came along.

"If you think you're gonna find it in North Karagi, or even South Karagi, then you're more delusional than I thought."

Our arguments became worse as the day of his departure approached. I was as much responsible as he was as we hurled accusations at each other. I guess because we're guys it never occurred to us to discuss our feelings and why we were constantly sniping at each other. I wouldn't have had a clue anyway.

I guess Reed was always at the back of my mind. I wondered how he was doing, whether he found himself a girlfriend or whether he was fucking himself senseless with a different chick every week. Surprisingly, Vic, the group's nominal head honcho heard about Reed every now and then because his older brother also attended the same university. The information was never anything really personal, just what he was doing around the campus – sweet FA by the sounds of it – and how he was doing exam wise – brilliantly as it turned out. I admit I was envious. I'll also admit I missed him. Maybe it was the fun times I missed, the lack of responsibility before I was saddled with a marriage.

You can tell by my phraseology that the marriage was not made in heaven; it was made much lower down. The birth of our daughter, Connie, didn't help. In fact, it made things worse. Home life was a constant screaming match, usually accusations flung at me when I got home from work, tired and hungry, that I was a shit provider for Stacey and the baby. I hated my home life. I hated my job. Reed's dad was right. The writing was on the wall, but everyone in the town had been lulled into complacency so when the first redundancy notices were handed out we were so shell-shocked that the world seemed to have spun off its orbit, we failed to organize.

Reed's dad tried to rally us but we were more like zombies, believing the platitudes about a hiccup in the economic fabric and to remain calm until an upturn in the market which would occur any day now. It wasn't until the second and third waves of redundancies were notched up that we began to question the validity of information the company was handing out. We'd been fed a steady diet of bullshit for so long we'd become addicted to it. It was difficult not to believe the comfortable propaganda the factory put out via the extremely well-paid PR firm employed to polish the company's reputation.

I was in the second group to go and with my job and my pay packet went my wife and child. They moved in with the executive who fired me ("Nothing personal," he said as he handed me my termination), while I moved back in with my parents. I stopped feeling guilty about my lack of ability to pay for my daughter's maintenance when my dad took me aside and explained the rumors that had circulated about the then married executive and Stacey around the time we wed. My guilt disappeared, although I was pissed off with my dad that he'd kept vital information from me.

Dad shrugged. "I thought you loved her, son."

When Stacey complained about my lack of economic support, I pointed out that (a) I had no income apart from unemployment benefits, and (b) if she went to the courts for a share of my redundancy pay-out I would insist on a paternity test for my daughter. Stacey was talked into letting it drop by her new boyfriend who was going through a painful divorce of his own from a wife who was looking for any excuse to hit him hard for any peccadillos she could uncover. In the end she must have seen some resemblance between her former husband and Connie because the court ordered the test which proved I was not Connie's dad.

I'd been unemployed for the best part of eight months during which time I looked for employment anywhere I could find it. I picked up odd jobs here and there but I was woefully unskilled for anything other than assembly-line factory work in an era when that sort of employment was being outsourced to overseas.

At my lowest point, I was seated with other guys from the gang in one of the cafés that didn't mind the unemployed sitting on a single cup of coffee all day as long as business was quiet. The boss there understood how dispiriting it was to sit at home with nothing to do and even fewer prospects. Depression can be self-perpetuating.

Les, one of the more upbeat members of the group waved a leaflet in our faces as a cheer-up. "Look, guys, time to get those frocks out of the closet and dry cleaned. The Little Black Dress Fun Run is coming up."

None of us could get enthused about the event under the circumstances.

"I think I'll give it a miss this year," Glen yawned.

"Me, too," I said.

There was a general murmur of agreement from around the table as we went back to our card game, played for matches.

"Come on, guys." Les attempted to gee us up without much success. "Where's your civic pride. We can't let South Karagi shit all over us."

For the past ten years there'd been good-natured rivalry between north and south over the event, held for charity every year. It wasn't just our two towns that participated, people came from all over, but the run began in our town and the finish line was twelve kilometers away in South Karagi, the course winding around the coast road to make the race just that little bit more painful. It had begun as just a normal race for people who wanted the fun of a Sunday morning event but professional mini-marathon competitors threatened to take it over and ruin the family-style atmosphere which saw everyone from babies in strollers to grannies in wheelchairs attempt the course. Although the event raised serious money, it was meant as fun for the participants.

To prevent people from taking it too seriously and to discourage the fitness gate crashers, the organizers hit on the idea of everyone wearing a black frock and high heels. Some men baulked at the idea, voicing their opinion that a drag race was just too, too gay, until their initial reluctance was overcome when they saw the outrageous fun the participants had in the early years. Men donned black dresses over their jeans at first until it became almost de rigueur to strip down to just their undies and show as much hairy cleavage in a black frock that would have had them arrested if a woman dared wear it to a bar. The high heels proved an impediment to the men winning hands down and it was usually a woman who won each year.

Some men took to practicing wearing stilettos secretly at home, while some took to wearing wigs that looked like something you'd find on Norman Bates's mum. Sure, a few glamour drag queens came up from the city to participate but they were also the after-race entertainment at the pub near the finishing line. The pub was gay on weekends, but for one Sunday a year it opened its doors to any gender that participated in the race.

The first year our mob attended, we were nervous about mingling but it was the only pub allowed to open on a Sunday morning, plus the drinks were cheap and the drag queen entertainment, once we got used to it, amazing. Married men with kids would pop in for a quick beer and then scuttle away before the rowdy and raucous show started. Others would pack their wife or girlfriend to the upstairs bar where kids were allowed in a designated area while dad boozed away downstairs. Blind eyes were turned on that one day of the year and it was the proverbial 'good time was had by all.'

Some of the behavior in the bar and, especially, in the men's toilet took a bit of getting used to but innocent cock sucking through a glory hole in the cubicle wall or a smidgen of butt fucking in the alley behind the pub was not something to particularly concern ourselves over. As long as the gay boys left us alone, it was cool, although a few of the straight guys went home miffed that they didn't at least get hit on or their butt pinched.

"What's wrong with me?" Les moaned one year. "Am I not good enough for these gay guys?" He was placated later when a chubby drag queen came down off stage and cooed "What's your name, handsome?" at him into the microphone. That made his day.

Glen took the leaflet for the event from Les and stared at it as if it might bring him good luck. "I suppose it'll give us something to look forward to."

"Doesn't cost anything," Les agreed.

"Drinks at the end," I reminded him.

"Maybe we can find a sugar daddy to shout us a round," Graeme suggested half-seriously.

Glen laughed. "It's your ass on the line."

"Speaking of which," Les whispered leaning across the table as if he was about to impart secret information. "The other day just as I was about to pump a load up my Trudy's twat, she suddenly shoves her finger up my date. Bugger me if she doesn't hit this spot inside my ass that sends sparks to my brain and I came buckets and saw stars."

Glen's reaction was immediate. "Ewww."

"She hit your prostate," I said knowingly. That raised a few eyebrows. "I saw a program on the telly about it. It's the male G-spot or something."

The guys looked uncomfortable so I let it drop. Les had gone the color of beetroot and was obviously sorry he'd brought up the subject.

Conversation took a back seat to the cards for a while after that. The charity fun run was a little over two weeks away. When I went home that afternoon to my parents who could not understand why I didn't find a job even if it meant cleaning toilets, I wanted to scream at them that I wasn't even qualified to do that. Later, I locked myself in my bedroom for privacy before I scrounged through my meager supply of clothes until I found the cocktail frock scrunched up at the back of the wardrobe.

Held up against my body, it looked as if it might still fit, although it was wrinkled and had a tear in one of the seams. What the hell, I stripped down to my underwear and shucked the dress over my head wriggling into it, pulling the hem down until I could admire myself in the mirror. Admire is too strong a word. I could never pass as a woman in a million years but that wasn't the point. Looking at myself like that made me smile. I found the shoes and, perched in my high heels, I tried walking around the bedroom until I fell on the bed my legs aching from the effort. I'd need to get in some practice. I'd also need to lose a couple of kilos because the dress was tight around my belly. Too much sitting down.

One by one over the coming week most of us signed up for the run, getting sponsors, shaking out our old wigs, and practicing running in stilettos. It increased our self-worth to be actually doing something constructive other than playing cards. The effect on the group was gratifying.

It was a week out from the event when Vic joined us at the café. He'd found work of a sort at a servo that was a glorified convenience store-cum-gas station; night shift manager because he was a hulking bastard whose looks frightened off anyone who thought the place was easy pickings.

"Hey, guys," he greeted us, high fiving around the booth in which we were seated. "Guess who's gonna join us this year for the fun run?"

We all made suggestions from Kylie Minogue to the Dalai Lama but we weren't even close.

Vic smirked. At that moment I knew what he was about to say and the bottom fell out of my stomach. "Reed is coming back to town. He's gonna join us for the Little Black Dress Fun Run."

"Shit, man, what's up?" Glen asked.

"He's finished his degree and he's coming home."

I had to ask. "For good?"

Vic looked at me suspiciously. Whether it was because my face had gone deathly pale or because of the catch in my voice, I wasn't sure. "Nah, to see his parents now he's graduated. He's gonna pack everything up and he's off."

I was grateful to Les when he asked, "Where's he going?"

"Dunno. You can ask him when he gets back. He's due day after tomorrow."

"Maybe we should throw him a party," Graeme suggested.

Glen seemed concerned. "What if he doesn't want to know us?"

Vic was puzzled. "Why would you think that?"

"He didn't turn up for Thom's wedding and they were the best of mates."

"Probably busy with exams," I said in his defense.

Glen wasn't going to let it rest. "He didn't send a wedding present either."

I had to think fast. "Stacey and I knew how poor students are and we told him not to worry."

"Not what Stacey told me," Glen said triumphantly. "She was really pissed off. She was expecting something pretty spectacular from your best buddy."

"Drop it, will you!" I snapped.

The gang stared at me in surprise but changed the subject. I excused myself as soon as possible and walked home. The 'fresh' air did nothing to clear my head and I was even more agitated as I walked into the house, swapping insults with my mum when she asked where I'd been all day. I had to get a grip.

It wasn't much better the next day so I avoided people as much as possible, preferring my own company. The day after, the buzz went around town that Reed was back home with his parents and was going to be at the ad hoc party Les had organized at his parents' place because they were away for the week and had plenty of food and grog we could raid.

I arrived late, deliberately, to avoid embarrassment. Most of the guys would be three sheets to the wind before I sneaked in via the back door. The sounds of laughter and shouting in the living room coupled with loud music covered my entrance but, wouldn't you know it, Reed was in the kitchen as I opened the back screen door to slip inside.

He saw my reflection in the kitchen window as he was facing away from me pouring himself a drink. His reflected eyes met mine. "For a while I thought you weren't coming."

I had a lie prepared but he'd see through it, so I shrugged.

He finished topping up his glass before turning and leaning back against the sink while he sipped his drink.

"Looking good, Thom," he said.

I snorted at the very idea. I did have to admit, though, that he looked spectacular. The years away had changed him. He was remarkably handsome, long hair suited him, and his body was packed tightly into jeans that hugged his curvy ass and prominent bulge. The tight T-shirt highlighted his muscle tone. I realized I was staring. "You, too."

"I was sorry to hear about you and Stace," he said.

"You didn't come to the wedding." I failed to keep some of the bitterness out of my voice.

"You didn't come to see me off."

I shrugged. "I didn't know it was that important to you."

"Sure you did. You didn't come because Stacey gave you an ultimatum."

He waited for my confirmation but when it wasn't forthcoming, even though it was true, he continued. "She was using you, Thom. To get back at the guy she really wanted. It took a couple of years but she got her way."

"Bit late telling me now."

"I thought you'd wake up to the truth eventually."

"I did."

"Which truth would that be?" he asked, a cheeky grin lighting his face.

I was puzzled by the question. "What do you mean?"

"Did you think about me during the past four years?"

I was offended by the question. "Of course, I did." I couldn't bring myself to ask him the same question. I was scared of the answer, either way. He must have read it in my features because he answered anyway.

"Every single day, Thom."

I was uncomfortable, so I changed the subject. "I hear you came back for the Little Black Dress Charity Run."

"For old time's sake. I hope you're going to be there."

"Wouldn't miss it for quids."

He shifted as one of the guys came into the kitchen to get a beer, and somehow managed to steer me into the comparative privacy of the back yard. We both leaned against a brick retaining wall at the edge of the back garden gazing back at the house. It was warm, possibly because Reed was standing uncomfortably close to me. Neither of us looked at each other. Silence had never been a problem between us before but this night it stretched until I was uncomfortable.

"I've grown up a great deal in the past four years, Thom," Reed said finally.

I wasn't sure what he was getting at, so I just nodded and muttered "Mmmm?" as I took a sip of my drink.

He continued. "Done a lot of thinking. Learned a lot about myself, about life."

I had my opening. "I hear you've got a job waiting for you in the city."

"Anything is better than this shit hole," he spat, raising my hackles by the way he disparaged my home town.

"It's not that bad," I protested.

"It's suffocating here," he said.

"That's a bit harsh. You haven't been here in four years. Not even to see your parents."

It was an accusation he brushed aside easily. "They came to visit me. They preferred it that way."

I don't know what made me ask. "You got a steady girl friend?" Even stranger was the feeling of relief that flooded through me when he replied that he hadn't.

"I am in love though," he added.

That stung for some reason.

I tried being sympathetic but it came out as smug. "She doesn't love you?"

He shrugged. "I don't know."

"You haven't told her?" I was amazed.

"That's why I came back."

"She's somebody from North Karagi? You sly dog. When are you going to tell her?" I was curious to know who it was at the same time I felt sick to my stomach over the news.

"It's hopeless," he said.

"What? She's married or something?"

"No, dickwad. Are you really so thick?"

I'd been called stupid, thick, idiot all my life so I was flustered when Reed said it. As a result I missed his sudden movement when he pressed his lips against mine. I must have opened my mouth in surprise for the next thing I knew he had his tongue inside and I felt his hard cock pressed against my crotch. For an instant I responded, pressing back against him, welcoming his heat into my own mouth. Then I snapped out of it, shoving him hard in the chest so he fell on his ass on the lawn.

"What's the matter with you?" I shouted.

He picked himself up with all the dignity he could muster, brushed his clothes down, faced me with sadness in his eyes, "I should never have come back. I knew it was a mistake. My apologies, Thom. My mistake."

I almost spluttered in indignation. "What made you think I was a fag?"

"I was hoping."

The penny dropped. "You're in love with me?"

"I think I have been all my life," he replied. "It was only when you didn't turn up at the station to see me off I realized something wasn't quite right with my life. When you married Stacey it ripped my heart out. When I heard about your divorce, I'm sorry, but I cheered. It meant I might have a chance. It might even mean you'd come to the same truth I had. It seems not."

He turned and walked back into house. I was so shocked I remained in the backyard, my head whirling at his revelation, wondering what the hell I'd ever done to make him think I was gay. I finished my drink and left the party.

I didn't see Reed again or speak to him until the day of the Little Black Dress Fun Run. I'd spent three sleepless nights trawling back through our mutual past to see if I could detect where we'd gone from bromance to gaymance. I could see that we were really close and sometimes we were on the borderline between gay men and straight men, but I couldn't detect that we'd ever crossed over. Then why had I felt so bad choosing to stay with Stacey instead of seeing him off to university? Why had it hurt he didn't come to my wedding or at least send his congratulations? Most of all, why did my belly do a backflip when I heard he was coming back to town? I wasn't sure I wanted the answers.

I almost withdrew from the fun run but Vic and the gang turned up to give me a lift. They wouldn't take no for an answer, insisting they would strip and frock me if I didn't do it myself. That was threat enough. I looked ridiculous but that was the point. As I didn't want any fag coming on to me, I deliberately butched it up so everyone would recognize my hetero bona fides.

In the car ride to the starting line the guys did not stop about Reed and what a great guy he was, etc. etc. etc. until I wanted to scream at them to shut the fuck up. Instead I hummed, creating white noise in my head to drown out their conversation. Unfortunately, I would have had to pluck out my eyes to have avoided Reed when we got to the starting line where families and friends were congregating with an air of expectation.

We went to the counter to register. I noticed Reed already had a number pinned to the back of his frock which drew attention to his ass. I also noticed – how could you miss it? – Reed had dressed to thrill. He'd obviously shaved his legs and his torso because his arms and chest were smooth and tanned. With his long hair he was stunning. There was no doubting he was male but the tight black cocktail dress that barely covered the curve of his butt also highlighted his pecs so they almost appeared like small breasts, and his legs were so gorgeous you couldn't help but think heaven was lodged between them. He'd teased his hair a little to give it body so it looked feminine, but it was the red lipstick that drew attention to his pouty mouth. I shivered when I imagined what those lips could do to a man.

Before I realized what I was doing, I ran my thumb across my own lips remembering the feel of Reed's mouth against my own. Reed, who seemed to be entertaining a group of obviously gay men, looked up and saw me. He nodded, smiling at catching me with my thumb caressing my lips. At least he didn't notice my cock hardening beneath my black sheath. I hoped my two pairs of undies would keep it trapped.

"Oh my God, how hot is Reed?" Vic said after he'd finished signing on and noticed at whom I was staring. He nudged the others in the group to watch as Reed made his way over to us, slithering provocatively, or so I thought, obviously to taunt me.

"I think I could change for you," Les admitted with a wink.

Vic squeezed Reed's ass affectionately. "I could so easily fuck that."

"Why makes you think I wouldn't be fucking you?" Reed replied, patting Vic's cheeks.

Vic surprised me when he said quite brazenly, "As long as you wear your high heels and your lipstick you can do with me what you like."

The gang laughed but I sensed the dynamic had changed. Sure we used to horse around in years past, even when Reed was here, but this was more than joking; this was some serious flirting.

Reed threw his arms around Vic's neck and kissed him on the cheek leaving an imprint of prominent red lips which he wore as a badge of pride. Reed also rubbed his body against Vic who clasped his ass grinding him closer. I wasn't the only one to notice the tent in Vic's frock.

"Wipe that shit off your mouth," I snapped. "You look like a tramp."

Reed laughed at me and I could smell alcohol on his breath. "Don't tell me what to do, Thom. You're not my boyfriend, much as you'd like to be…"

I spluttered in fury unable to string two coherent words together. The others laughed at my discomfort. I knew if I stormed off now it would be worse for me later, so I bit my tongue and pretended to join in the joke.

I watched Reed who seemed to be flaunting himself like a cheap hussy at any man whose interest he piqued. The gang was very taken with Reed's new look. I didn't take the time to analyze my antagonism because we were herded to the marshaling area and waved off in groups. Most people just walked the twelve kilometers, while others such as us trotted precariously on high heels in an attempt at speed. I was amazed at Reed's dexterity in heels wondering where he'd learned the skill; the rest of us were finding it difficult to keep up.

Because he was ahead of us we all had an opportunity to ogle his fine ass which I'm sure he was swishing in a deliberately provocative manner to entice us. If this was his revenge for my rejection of his advances, it wasn't going to work. At least I hoped if I kept repeating that over and over to myself it might become true.

People lined the streets along the route cheering us on, whistling at our outfits or else handing out bottles of water so we didn't get too dehydrated. There was little to no chance to socialize on the run as we sped toward the pub where we'd celebrate our daring until all hours of the night.

A little under two and a half hours later we staggered across the finishing line, nowhere near the runners who'd finished first, but with a larger number behind us than had been in front. All of us except Reed kicked our high heels off, our feet blistered from the unfamiliar footwear, and walked barefoot into the pub. They turned a blind eye on an occasion like this and in deference to our naked and aching feet served alcohol in plastic cups.

Because we were among the middle of the pack to arrive first we managed to get ourselves a booth in the pub, ensconcing ourselves happily in order to get pissed while we watched the drag show which was due to start in a couple of hours, once the stragglers crossed the line. By that time we'd be very merry indeed. Reed was in the middle of the semi-circular padded seat hemmed in by Vic and Glen. I was disgusted as they were treating him as if he were a piece of meat. Vic, in particular, had his paws all over Reed's hot body.

I don't know whether it was my look of disapproval but I was sent off to buy a pitcher of beer and bring back enough plastic cups to go around. By the time I returned from the bar, members of the gang were whooping it up, reminiscing about some of our more outrageous exploits of the past. As I listened I wondered where those wild carefree boys had gone. Glancing around the table all I saw now were the faces of men ground down by the system, desperately trying to have a good time. All except Reed who seemed to be in his element.

The pub was filling with runners of all shapes and sizes, all togged out in little black frocks. It was quite a sight. After the second pitcher of beer, the pub owner announced that the kitchen was open for snacks to soak up all the alcohol. After a quick discussion it was decided we'd go for the fish and chips and share it around the table. It wasn't gourmet fare, rather it was crinkle cut chips along with deep-fried battered fish. It came in white butcher's paper with a couple of wedges of lemon, salt, and vinegar if you requested it.

We ordered and when our number was called, Les went to pick it up. The meal, spread out in the center of the table so we could all help ourselves, went perfectly with cold beer. What was important, it was filling and some of the guys burped their appreciation. I'd spent most of the time chatting to Graeme while keeping half an eye on Reed. He caught me, smirking his satisfaction so that I got irate enough to give him my best Robert De Niro impersonation – 'You lookin' at me?' - but common sense prevailed and I kept my mouth shut.

Vic and Reed were in very intimate conversation and I wondered what they found to talk about as they'd never been particularly close before. Because of the noise from the pub patrons it was impossible to hear what they were saying. Reed was looking very flushed, his hands beneath the table perilously close to where I assumed Vic's crotch would be, but I couldn't tell if the blush was from the alcohol or Vic running his hands all over Reed's body.

When it was announced the floor show would be commencing in half an hour, we were already on our fifth or sixth pitcher of beer. I knew enough to head to the men's room to relieve my bladder because the place would be packed shortly. There was a line inside so I had to wait my turn for the urinals or one of the cubicles to become vacant. Not long after I entered I was surprised to see Reed come in. He didn't acknowledge or even look at me but rather went to the basin to refresh his lipstick and, to my horror, began to remove his underpants so he was commando style under his short frock. A number of men in the rest room watched in fascination as he pulled the skirt down over his ass and patted his bulge at the front. I was afraid his balls would poke out below the hemline.

A number of men whispered what were obviously pick-up lines in his ear, a number of them thrusting scribbled phone numbers at him. He took them all with a smile and a pleasant word. Whether he was being polite or intended following up on them I couldn't judge. Either way, I was sick to my stomach at his behavior.

By the time I finished my ablutions and got back to the table, Graeme had moved beside Reed although Vic was still hogging the other side. I toyed with the idea of going home before the show started but that would have been ill-mannered. Besides, I loved the drag shows, they were best part of the day.

The leftover chips were cooling in the center of the table when Reed stood up to reach across and grab a few of the remaining slabs of deep-fried potato. He seemed unsteady on his feet, probably from all the beer he'd drunk, so Vic grabbed him around the waist to stop him falling. Reed propped himself against the table as he bent forward, the hem of his dress lifting up. Vic patted Reed's naked ass and I could have sworn he dipped a finger in his ass crack. I was even more convinced of it when I noticed a startled look on Reed's face before it relaxed into a smile of satisfaction. He remained bent over the table much longer than necessary in order to gather up the few remaining chips, his breathing ragged as his body shuffled forward as if he was being pushed.

I was about to remonstrate with Vic when the lights dimmed to signify the show was about to start and Reed sat down so abruptly he ended up in Vic's lap. It must have been uncomfortable because Reed wriggled about until he could find a comfortable position. From time to time during the show I glanced across at my former best friend who seemed to be wriggling with excitement at every mimed song and every joke. Just before the first interval I was shocked to look over to discover Reed was missing although Vic had his head thrown back, his mouth gaping, groaning almost loudly enough to be heard over the piped music.

My blood ran cold. Reed's head bobbed up from under the table as he wiped his mouth with the back of his hand. Both Vic and Reed saw me staring but acknowledged my scowl with smirks of satisfaction. I couldn't believe my best mate was a slut. I also couldn't believe I was hard as stone and felt queasy at Reed's behavior.

I didn't have time to dwell on it as the lights came up and the DJ began playing music to fill the void between the two halves of the show. The guys all piled onto the dance floor surrounding Reed who was the center of attention. I was nominated to mind the seat from poachers. At least I had a perfect view of what was going on in the middle of the dance floor. Reed was sandwiched between Glen in the front and Vic behind. Vic was quite openly grinding his crotch against Reed's naked butt after lifting the back of his short skirt.

The floor was crowded so I suspect most people had no idea what was going on, but between the dancing sweaty bodies I caught sight of Vic unzipping and hauling out his cock, aiming it at Reed's ass before thrusting forward.

I heard the yelp of surprise from where I was seated, watching as Reed attempted to escape the penetration but Glen held him captive. I saw red. I was up and out of my seat striding across the dance floor, pushing through the throng of dancers until I reached Vic to tap him on the shoulder. When he turned to see who was interrupting him, I fisted him on the jaw. He dropped like a sack of rice.

Glen obviously saw my look of anger and promptly let go of Reed; Graeme and Les also giving me a wide berth. I took Reed by the arm and hustled him off the dance floor and toward the door out onto the street.

"Hey," he yelled, struggling to free himself from my grip.

Perhaps he thought I was security or something because when he realized it was me, he relaxed. "Oh, it's you," he said.

"What's the matter with you? Haven't you got any self-respect?" I demanded.

"Ha," he shouted in my face. "What about you?"

I was puzzled. "What about me?"

"You've had a hard-on for me all night."

I went to object but it was no use.

He went on. "Is your erection for me or because of what the guys were doing to me?"

"We can talk about this when we get away from here," I said quietly. People were beginning to stare.

"No, we can discuss it here because, unless I get the right answers, I'm marching right back into the pub to continue where I left off."

"What was the question again?" I was trying to buy time in the hope I could bundle him in a taxi and get him out of there.

He answered by grabbing my cock through my dress. "Is this for me?"

"Yeah, it is," I admitted. "I'm not gay. Except I find I'm gay for you. It doesn't make sense—"

I didn't have a chance to say anything further because just then an empty cab drove past and Reed flagged him down. Pushing me into the back seat he gave the driver an address that was faintly familiar. When we pulled into the car park, I remembered. I looked at Reed, his face glowing with the memories.

We paid the driver, then Reed took my hand as he walked me across the sand dunes to the beach. It was a balmy evening, the sliver of moon just peeking above the horizon, stars beginning to twinkle in the darkening heavens.

"Remember this?" he said.

"Of course."

This was 'our' spot. We came here at night when the world was at our feet and we planned our future together.

"We were what?" I asked.

"Ten or eleven," he replied, flopping on the sand, his arms behind his head.

I sat beside him.

"We never expected it to end up like this," he laughed.

We were silent for a while before I dared broach the subject uppermost in my mind.

"Why did you let them treat you like a whore?"

He hesitated before he spoke. "I was trying to get a reaction out of you."

"You certainly achieved that. Was it the reaction you wanted?"

"Partly," he admitted. "The rest of it remains to be seen."

He looked so sweet, so vulnerable lying there in the sand with his eyes closed. I couldn't help it, I leaned over and placed my lips against his. I heard his sharp intake of breath before he opened up to allow me in. I took my time gently sucking his tongue, running mine around his teeth pushing into his warm wet mouth.

I felt like I was suffocating and pulled away to catch my breath.

"Wow," he said. "Where did you learn to kiss like that?"

"I didn't know I could kiss like that. It must be you."

I lay on the sand placing my arm under his head pulling him onto my chest.

"I can hear your heart beating," he said running his fingers through my hair.

We lay like that for quite a while, his fingers on my face, my hands caressing his lower back and rubbing over his butt cheeks.

He broke the silence. "Come with me, Thom. Leave Karagi, come to the city."

"What would I do?"

"What do you do here?"

He had a point.

"We'll find you a job. Meanwhile, I have a good paying position with an advertising agency. I can support us both. Plus I have a little money saved up."

"What will I be?"

"My friend. My boy friend."

"I don't know if I'm gay, Reed."

"You don't have to be. As long as you're gay for me."

He slid his hand under my frock and found my dick pulsating in my undies. He kneeled and lifted my skirt above my waist, pulling my briefs down under my balls. His hand around my shaft felt like an electrical charge through my body. When he put his mouth over the head of my prick I saw stars and they weren't all in the heavens above us.

An immense feeling of satisfaction washed over me. I could do this. Okay, the thought of reciprocation terrified me but, at the same time, excited me. I knew I was in safe hands with Reed. He made me feel fluttery in the stomach. He made me feel safe. He made me feel handsome and strong, not unemployed and useless. With him the future seemed littered with unlimited potential again. And he was the most beautiful man I had ever met.

That seemed enough to hang a dream on for now.

The Three Spooges

"Oh, it's a long long while from May to November," Larry sang, paraphrasing an old Broadway tune.

November was his favorite month of the year; the month in which hair started sprouting on the top lips of hot men all over the city. Movember they called it because men with a conscience grew a moustache to aid awareness of men's health issues. Not that Larry gave a shit about men's health or awareness. All he was interested in was his own sexual health – whether he was getting it or not – and indulging in his top fetish: men with a moustache.

Larry gave a portion of his salary to help support those with cancer, those with depression, and, especially, those living with HIV, but he didn't know anyone with cancer and the only depression he knew was that when Movember was over, men went back to shaving their top lip again. If only he could persuade the powers that be to make Movember a year-long event, he'd gladly give more of his hard-earned cash.

Especially this year, his twenty-seventh, when he'd found not one, but three eligible men he could easily make permanent if they gave him the opportunity. The one deciding factor would be if they decided to keep the fine strip of hair beneath their noses. He wasn't greedy, he didn't want all three, one was enough to settle down with. He'd heard of polyandry but that seemed like far too much trouble to make it worthwhile. He'd had trouble in the past just balancing a career and one lover. He shuddered at the thought of balancing more than that.

He wasn't especially good at relationships anyway, much as he wanted one. They all seemed to go pear-shaped somehow. Either he grew bored with the same old/same old or they dumped him for someone younger and hotter. It was beginning to get embarrassing. Most of his friends had settled into comfortable domesticity, leaving him the perennial unshagged on a rock. People began to look at him as if there was something seriously wrong with him. Here he was rapidly approaching thirty, yet unable to sustain a long-term relationship. There was a name for people like that: to his friends he was a slut, to other bar patrons he was a loser. At his age, anyone still cruising the bars looking for love must have a serious deficiency of some sort.

Larry was good-looking in that scrubbed face collegiate way of the eternal Peter Pans with a gym-toned body. There was nothing exceptional about him. On any given night at a gay bar he slotted into the mid-range in looks, body and cock size. He wasn't ugly, he wasn't ass-clenchingly hot. In a world of devastatingly hot men with bodies buffed to perfection, he was average. Take him out of the hothouse of competitive cruising, and Larry was a stunner. On a normal city street during working hours, Larry turned heads. He just never noticed because his head was always so far into his cell phone with its apps for all manner of sites to pick up men, he never looked up long enough to see the admiring glances.

Until the day he ran into – literally ran into…He'd noted the closest gay man looking for quick alley sex was one hundred meters ahead of him and he put on speed to catch up without looking where he was going. He was closing in fast because the distance between them was dropping with every step he took. The object of his pursuit must have seen his approach in his own phone and waited for him to catch up.

He was less than a block away when, absorbed by the proximity of his target and very pleased with himself, he barreled into a pedestrian who had attempted to sidestep a crowd surging to cross the road when the lights changed. Larry hit the ground, his phone clattered to the pavement, and then was kicked into the gutter by folk impatient to get to work. He scrambled after his precious phone only to be accidentally kicked himself, his hands crushed under shoes, his body bruised by hard physical contact until someone reached down, and pulled him to his feet.

Larry was about to tell his savior to mind his own business, his eyes still on the whereabouts of his phone, when a deep masculine voice enquired as to his welfare.

"Are you all right? No bones broken?"

Larry looked up, intrigued by the smooth, sonorous tones. He knew instantly he had met the man he wanted to spend the rest of his life with. The seventh one that week.

Tom had been hurrying as he was late for an appointment with a very important person. Well, the person concerned believed himself to be 'very important.' Tom was more likely to think of him as an 'asshole.' Clive had once been his business partner as well as his lover but they'd split up as romantic partners almost nine months before when Clive fell for the faded charms of his twink personal assistant, while overlooking the bleach-blond hair, the total lack of secretarial skills, and the personality bleached into near non-existence. They deserved each other.

The business partnership was terminal now; it had been hemorrhaging top clients for months. Tom had recently discovered the reason. Clive had quietly set up a shadow business and had begun secretly seducing the important business over to his side. It was borderline legal, but certainly immoral.

Grinding his teeth in an attempt to keep a lid on his temper, rehearsing all the things he wanted to say to his treacherous former partner but which would remain unspoken for the sake of civility, he wasn't concentrating on where he was going. He was oblivious to his surroundings and it wasn't until he felt the impact that he remembered he was in a public street. He managed to stay on his feet but the person with whom he'd collided was not so lucky, having fallen hard on his ass, his cell phone scooting across the pavement to the gutter. Tom quickly retrieved the phone which looked none the worse for the collision and was about to remonstrate that people should look where they were going when he glanced at his victim.

He couldn't help but smile as he extended his hand to help him up. "Are you all right?" he enquired. "No bones broken?"

The young man who took his hand seemed equally as grim and determined to milk the situation for as much mileage as he could. Tom had been prepared to do the same at first as the young man had obviously been far too engrossed in his phone to watch where he was walking. Now he was more than happy to brush the dust from the young man's clothes while apologizing profusely which had the unexpected effect of disarming both of them.

"You've got a moustache," the young man said, returning his smile.

Tom had forgotten all about his business meeting at that moment. He couldn't believe his luck. This was the very young man he'd been watching across a crowded bar last night, too timid to approach as he believed him way out of his league.

"Tom," he said.

"Larry."

"Let me buy you breakfast to make up for my clumsiness. Unless, of course, you feel you need to contact your lawyer, the hospital, or a television reality program. Or you have somewhere you have to be."

"That would be very pleasant," Larry replied. "I was merely following a…um…lead."

It wasn't until he switched on his own cell phone and got an ear bashing from his secretary, that Tom realized he'd missed his appointment. He also realized he'd been smiling for the past two hours as he got to know Larry.

He cut his secretary off with the startling news, "I think I've found the man I want to marry."

Larry placed the name card on the table. Tom had been a fixture in his life for the past three weeks and it was time they had 'the talk.' He was pretty sure Tom felt the same way he did but he had to broach the subject of the moustache because Tom had been complaining recently about how it itched and was looking forward to shaving it off.

Yes, Larry knew he was shallow but Tom's fine hair lip was the crowning glory on an otherwise just-shy-of-perfect man. This evening was to convince him to keep it for the sake of any future they might have together.

He was particularly happy as he'd prepared a perfect meal, all the ingredients freshly purchased from the new greengrocer's that had opened two blocks from his apartment. The area had been crying out for a fresh produce store, this one living up to the hype so that within weeks of its opening it had become an unprecedented success. A lot of that had to do with the gay men who packed the store, mainly on weekends, and that in turn, had a lot to do with Cary, the young student who worked the vegetable aisles, restocking leafy greens and earthy tubers, while parrying attempts to grope his privates and his ass, or deflect unwanted phone numbers and party invitations.

Larry had often seen the young assistant struggle to control his temper after yet another attempted pass from a customer. Once or twice, Larry had stepped in to diffuse a situation that threatened to develop into something very unpleasant by asking the whereabouts of something in the store or seeking an explanation as to the correct preparation of a particular vegetable dish. He had no erotic interest in the lad even though he was always friendly and seemed eager to chat whenever Larry came into the store. Sure, he was good-looking and had a slim, tight body from shooting hoops and touch football with his buddies, but he was lacking that something special that would have turned Larry into a slobbering predator: a moustache.

Even his disheveled emo hair, a style Larry normally detested, looked good on him but without the hairy lip he was as sexually alluring as a concrete driveway. It was all for the best because Cary complained long and loud about the ugly propositions he received hourly from men in whom he had absolutely no interest. Larry commiserated as best he could while thinking there were probably worse things than popularity. He didn't know because he'd never felt the envious and lustful stares from men in the street – he was oblivious to anyone without the necessary moustache.

Their relationship had settled into a happy chatty acquaintanceship until late October, until the day Larry walked into the fruit boutique and discovered a dark smudge under Cary's nose.

"What is that?" Larry laughed.

"Protection," Cary admitted.

"Protection?"

"The boss has allowed me to grow a moustache for charity during Movember. He doesn't usually like facial hair but because it's for a worthy cause…" he shrugged.

Leaning in to whisper conspiratorially, he added, "Besides it turns off a lot of the gay guys. They prefer their twinks to be hairless. So for an entire month I'll be left alone."

Cary didn't understand what was going on. Larry, one of the few gay guys who hadn't attempted to crawl up his ass from the moment the shop opened was avoiding him. Since the day he'd begun growing hair on his upper lip he'd seen Larry watching him from the end of the aisles but never coming anywhere near him. He wondered what he'd done. Had he inadvertently insulted him? Said something he shouldn't? He missed his talks with the slightly older man. He thought they were friends of a sort even though their socializing had taken place within the four walls of the greengrocer's shop. Now it was as if he had some terrible contagious disease.

For two weeks Larry had avoided him, even turning up on Cary's days off. His aisle buddy, Claudine, said she'd noticed Larry had changed his shopping routine now preferring her expertise to his. Hurt and anxious, determined to get to the bottom of the cold shoulder, Cary decided to lie in wait on his next rostered day off.

Damn it, he liked Larry. Really liked him. At first he thought it was because Larry treated him with respect, didn't invade his personal space, didn't grope his ass when he turned his back. Larry was funny, Larry was interesting and took the time to ask about his life and his interests. Unfortunately, his interests over the past few months had mainly been Larry and how to ask him out on a date. The older man seemed so confident and self-contained. It was maddening that Cary got so flustered and awkward every time Larry entered the store.

He was close to summoning up the courage to invite Larry to a concert by his favorite rock band, a group they both admitted to liking, when that blight on his top lip ruined everything. Cary couldn't work out what it was about the spindly hairs that changed everything so drastically; he was still the same person underneath. A few hairs shouldn't make that much difference.

He wasn't prepared to write off their burgeoning friendship just yet; at least not until he had an explanation.

Cary watched from his hiding place as Larry entered the store. He didn't want to spook the man and cause a scene in his place of employment. He'd wait until Larry emerged with his shopping which would slow him down and make it much more difficult to make his escape. Timing it perfectly, Cary walked toward the sliding glass doors at the entrance as Larry emerged laden with bags of produce.

"Oh, hi," Cary beamed although his heart was pounding. Larry's eyes went straight to his newly minted moustache before a look of panic took over. Cary was quicker, suggesting, "Here, let me help you with those."

Before Larry could bolt, Cary had quickly relieved him of a number of bags so that he'd lose half his groceries if he ran.

"Thanks, but it's really not necessary," Larry said with a slight tremor to his voice.

"No trouble," Cary said cheerfully, walking alongside in the direction of Larry's car. He looked sideways at the man who was doing everything to avoid him, surprised to notice a thickening in the front of Larry's jeans.

It hadn't occurred to Cary that Larry might have developed a crush on him. Maybe Larry had found a boyfriend. He'd always said he was single and looking. Maybe he wasn't on the market any more. Cary was determined to find out, so when they arrived at the car and Larry put down his bags to fumble with his remote security device, Cary pushed him up against the car, gripping Larry's throbbing erection through his jeans. He'd never been so bold in all his twink years as to grope an older man. He didn't approve of such behavior when men did it to him but he could think of no other way to get straight to the point.

"Is that for me?"

Larry swallowed nervously but made no effort to push him away. That made him even bolder and he leaned in for the kiss he'd wanted more than anything.

If the older man would not take the initiative then he would. Cary was surprised when Larry not only opened his mouth to welcome the invading tongue but also wrapped his arms about him almost squashing out all his breath.

When they finally broke for air, they both had that startled headlights-like stare.

"I was beginning to think you didn't like me," Cary admitted.

"God, no. I was beginning to like you too much. Especially after you started growing your mo." For a brief moment, Larry was embarrassed. "You see, I have a thing for moustaches."

Cary cut off any further explanation by pasting his mouth over Larry's. He was grateful it was his day off.

That first afternoon had been sheer heaven. They'd spent hours in bed exploring each other's bodies until they knew just about every wrinkle, every dimple, and every hair. Larry had been so turned on he'd almost licked Cary's face off in his eagerness to get at the moustache. They'd been almost inseparable since. When Larry broached the subject of the all-important lip overgrowth to Cary, he'd revealed that it would probably have to go as he was an actor, working in the greengrocer to make ends meet, and not all casting agents like their men hairy. At the end of Movember it was likely to be all over for Larry if his newest boyfriend had to shave.

He was grateful he'd sneaked away to visit Tom while Cary was at work.

He placed Cary's name card on the table next to Tom's.

That would have been the end of it if his computer hadn't frozen five days ago. As a web designer, his computer was his lifeblood. Forget that he spent too many hours on Facebook trawling for inspiration in the form of hot men's naked asses and fulsome top lips. It was late in the evening when it occurred and his screen froze on a message from the Federal Police informing him he had been caught attempting to access an illegal website. He felt guilty for about thirty seconds as he read through the dire warning of fines and imprisonment and the fact his computer was frozen until the cops broke down his door and carted him off screaming.

Then his attention was drawn to the side panel in which he was instructed to immediately visit the nearest convenience store and send off one hundred dollars to have his computer unblocked. Yeah, right. Like the cops were freezing computers before recommending a cheap way of unblocking them. He relaxed. He would have known it was a scam if he hadn't been so intent on ogling men's rears.

It's not that he couldn't afford one hundred dollars; he could. He just objected to paying good money to scammers. Larry had been left comparatively well off by his late uncle Symon in whose spacious apartment he now lived. He had been close to his uncle and in the last years of his terminal illness was the only member of the family who visited. Even Larry's own mother – Symon's younger sister – had disowned the reprobate sibling. Larry sat and listened to his uncle's stories for hours, swapping celebrity gossip right up until the end. It was Symon who encouraged Larry to accept his fetish and revel in it. Until that time he'd kept his secret closeted. Larry had expected no recompense for the hours he'd spent at the apartment; he had accepted it as his duty to stay over on the night's his uncle's condition deteriorated. Larry never complained, the gay history lesson he received in return was ample reward.

Symon's wealth from writing scandalous airport paperback books remained a secret from friends and family right up to the reading of the will at which time Larry discovered he was set for life. Apart from a few bequests to friends and a number of charities mainly connected with his uncle's illness, Larry had been left the remainder, including the luxury apartment. The royalties to Symon's potboilers trickled in but he could not rely on that to sustain him but not having to worry about rent was a godsend. Utilities were another matter altogether.

He had a skill with computers which meant he could work from home; no more negotiating peak hour travel or having to mix with worker Neanderthals. So a little thing like a frozen computer could be sorted out in no time. At nine o'clock that night he conceded defeat. His expertise, his cursing, his security, his banging the desk all failed to impress the hacker. He had an urgent job to complete and although he wisely had a secondary computer for such emergencies, all the relevant information was behind his frozen screen.

The first few nerds he rang greeted his request with sneering laughter and an accusation he'd been trawling for illegal visual stimulation and deserved to rot in hell. He was about to admit defeat when he discovered a small advert tucked away, almost as if in embarrassment at its unprepossessing circumstances, at the bottom of the page of the local business directory. Larry almost discarded it. He'd tried all the big companies so why would a small one-man operation by the looks of it want his business. He thought of what the loss of this job would mean to his rapidly depleting bank balance and dialed the cell phone number. He was surprised when it was answered, equally surprised when the friendly guy at the other end said it would be no trouble to look at the problem that very evening without making a crack about morality and, even more surprisingly, quoted an hourly rate that he could afford without selling a kidney or a lung.

If the repair was satisfactory and the nerd as sexy as his voice, he would have no hesitation in recommending him to his friends and design acquaintances. The second part of the equation was answered the moment he opened the door. Richard was scruffy but clean. He smelled of hamburger and fries which he'd admitted to stopping for on his way over as he hadn't eaten. He thanked Larry profusely for his offer of a coffee, although Larry would have been glad to offer a blow job, a fuck, a weekend in Paris, anything to inveigle Richard into his bed, for the repair man had the cutest fuzz on his chin and lips, plus the most adorable looks and the deepest blue eyes…well, he could have gone on for days about Richard. Larry loved dick, and this Dick in particular.

"So, you're an ass man?" Richard asked as he packed away his discs and his computer paraphernalia after fixing the problem.

Larry blushed. He'd forgotten the virus must have entered his computer via the Butt Privates website. He'd gain nothing by prevaricating. "Only men's asses."

Richard smiled. "Yours is pretty hot. Is it on here?"

By the time Richard left the apartment the next morning he'd inserted not only his finger into Larry's butt, but also his tongue and his very thick and very hard cock – more than once. Larry felt dilated enough he could give birth. What was even more pleasing was that Richard took the time to update the security on Larry's machine, explained the scam to him, and offered to return the next night to ensure his computer was working satisfactorily.

It meant rejigging his schedule. He'd fobbed off Tom for one night on the pretext of a headache and rescheduled Cary for two hours earlier although he knew there was no way he could keep up the hectic schedule of pleasuring three men without killing himself; but what a way to go.

Richard returned the following night to check all was well but, in reality, hoping to spend another evening, if not night, buggering the ass off the hottest man he'd bedded in so long he couldn't remember. He wasn't even sure he'd ever had a man as lovable as Larry before. He was so tempted by him, Richard thought about planting his own virus in the computer so Larry had to ring him on a weekly basis. Maybe even ask him to move in.

He was barely able to pay for his vermin-ridden slum flat which is why his advert in the press was so… well…cheap. It was all he could afford. With the money he made from Larry's job he'd be secure for a few more weeks but he was in real danger of being turfed out on the streets, his computer confiscated for back rent. In the past he'd allowed a few men to take advantage of his youth and scruffy good looks for economic advantage and he was close to calling some of them to see if they were interested in a repeat performance.

He liked Larry, though. There was no charge for sex. He hoped he could keep on seeing Larry but Richard suspected the man was so far out of his league. For starters, Richard was scruffy. He'd tried to grow a beard and moustache but all he'd managed was the pretense. He had been told he'd get more work if he just scrubbed up; tidied himself up a little, beginning with a shave. He'd been on the verge of doing just that when Larry's lifeline call had come through. He was glad now he hadn't arrived with a smooth face as Larry seemed inordinately fond of that sparse fuzz on his face.

The second night had been even better than the first. He had turned up with his favorite passion fruit cheesecake as desert although they didn't stop to sample it until the early hours of the morning by which time they were sated with each other and ravenous for something sweet. The sugar rush kept them up until the sun rose in the morning by which time they'd made out for almost eight hours.

When Larry invited him back for the third and fourth nights running, he couldn't believe his luck. Larry had also been true to his word and recommended him to his friends so that work began to pick up slowly. At this rate he might snag himself a sustainable wage and, more importantly, a boyfriend.

Hoping for an invitation to stay over on the fifth night, Richard was delighted to receive an invitation to dine with Larry and two of his friends. That was a good sign, wasn't it? Larry showing off Richard to the people he cared about most?

Larry placed Richard's name card next to his own.

If anyone had asked him to make a choice between the three men he would have been hard-pressed to choose, although he favored Richard but only because his moustache was a permanent fixture and not something squatting on his face for a single month in aid of a charity.

The three men were as distinct in personality and sexual technique as was the taste of their spooge. Larry would be able to identify the men in the dark just by sucking their cocks. Not that he thought that idea would find favor with them. He was, however, willing to take a chance on happiness with one of them by laying his cards on the table. His uncle had recommended brutal honesty if he wanted to find true happiness. Tomorrow was the first day of December; clean shaven faces would be back in vogue. Larry didn't want that as he'd fallen ever so slightly in love with each of the three men, having quelled his emotions until he satisfied himself they would keep their moustache to please him. He hoped that would not be an ask-too-far for one of them.

He'd invited all three to dinner. He'd prepared something special, selected nice wine without going overboard as he didn't want to rub anyone's nose in his uncle's expensive wine collection, and set the dining room up in a most seductive manner. He hoped his new lovers wouldn't be pissed off with his rather outrageous behavior. Movember was his Christmas and he'd been a greedy boy this year.

Larry was more nervous than he ever had been before in his life. It's not like any of them had discussed fidelity, love or exclusivity during their weeks or days of lovemaking. It had been more than sex for Larry with all three of them, but how to explain his unconventional fetish. He was tired of one-night stands and was looking for something more permanent but his needs were specific and he wasn't about to commit to the first opportunity that presented itself. There were probably hundreds of…

The buzzer broke into his thoughts and he opened the door to Tom and Richard who'd met in the lift, surprised to discover they were both headed to the same destination. They were chatting animatedly like they were old mates as Larry ushered them inside. A few alcoholic beverages loosened their tongues and their libidos even further as they waited for the last member of the party to arrive. Cary had rung earlier to report he had an audition and might be up to thirty minutes late. When he did finally arrive, Larry was disappointed to see he'd shaved off his moustache already.

Reading the look in his eyes, Cary said, "My agent insisted it go for the audition. It was no matter as my boss at the store told me there'd been complaints from some members of the public who thought I looked too scruffy with it. Probably disgruntled gay guys who I wouldn't let touch me up."

Larry was the perfect host and didn't allow his displeasure at Cary's denuding to spoil the evening. The wine flowed, lubricating the conversation which Larry managed to steer away from any dangerous subject matter whenever it threatened, and the three men who had just met were getting along fine. In fact, Larry noticed a spark between Cary and Tom. This pulled him up short. He hadn't allowed for the others to feel sexual attraction to anyone but himself.

He broke the news during desert, a magnificent crème brûlée he had spent an inordinate amount of time preparing hoping to lull his guests into a sense of sated lethargy so they'd be loath to expend too much energy protesting his behavior. He misjudged badly and accusations flew across the table with the ferocity of the temper tantrums to which they gave vent. The three men had accepted his admission of a moustache fetish with equanimity because they'd guessed as much or he'd already told them, but his sexual gluttony was too much for them all, especially Richard who seemed devastated by the news. Larry was sorry he'd upset him, and determined he'd make it up somehow.

The evening threatened to deteriorate into shouting and tears until Cary broke into a fit of giggles which he could not control. His eyes watered, he held his belly as it threatened to split with laughter. His appalled fellow dinner guests could see little to laugh about until he spelled out the humor in the situation in between guffaws and belly laughs.

Richard was the last to succumb to the infectious good humor and allow himself to be led protesting to the bedroom where the four of them indulged their appetites in a leisurely fashion, sharing with each and every man until they paired off: Tom with Cary, Larry with Richard, although in the morning they swapped some more, agreeing it was a wonderful conclusion to a very interesting dinner. All but Richard, the only guest who seemed to harbor resentment and who took the earliest opportunity to leave, promising to keep in touch with everyone but without bothering to leave his details or take anyone else's.

Larry determined he would not let the young computer geek go without a fight. Richard it seemed had other ideas and in the following weeks refused to join any of the games in which the other three indulged. Larry was delighted when Cary got an acting job on a television series set in the 1890s and had to grow a bushy moustache for the role. The three friends became inseparable but Cary and Tom noticed Larry seemed to miss the fourth pillar of the group. Richard had not been in contact with any of them, refusing to return Larry's calls.

Christmas was rapidly approaching and the three of them were planning to spend time at Tom's cabin by a lake not two hours out of the city. They had only themselves to please and thoughts of a week together made Larry hard, although he was morose that Richard would be missing. He'd realized too late that he'd developed real feelings for him. Even leaving that admission on Richard's voice mail did not result in a return call.

Larry had a last-minute rush job to complete so would not arrive at the cabin until Christmas Eve. He was bringing the champagne and mince pies while Cary and Tom were supplying the other goodies. He was looking forward to the break. On the drive to the cabin he attempted to buck up his spirits by concentrating on the promise of hot sex with the other two men, especially as Cary's period moustache was beginning to take shape. The thought of that was enough to get him hard as hell, so he was humming as he turned off the main highway to take the dirt track to the edge of the lake.

His friends, happy to see him in a good frame of mind, welcomed him with hugs and kisses. They had committed to living together but without all the petty jealousies that sometimes accompanied relationships. They were happy to share with Larry. Tom would on occasions be away on business while Cary would sometimes be on location. It was understood that they were welcome, solo or in pairs at Larry's place, and vice versa, at any time.

Cory helped Larry carry the boxes of drinks and sweet Christmas puddings into the cabin. It had two bedrooms but the men were sleeping together in the large main bedroom upstairs. It was a hot, steamy southern hemisphere Christmas Eve, the sort that promised a late thunderstorm would roll in over the lake.

First, however, they wanted to get in a swim to cool off. They would have loved nothing better than to skinny dip but there were other cabins nearby and they didn't want to scare any holidaymakers in case they had children with them.

"I didn't think to bring a costume," Larry said.

Tom came to the rescue. "I have a spare or two in the second bedroom. Have a look in the closet. We're about the same size."

Tom was already out the door, racing down the dirt path to the wooden pier, hollering, "Last one in goes bottom tonight."

Cary took off after him leaving Larry clenching his buttocks in expectation of an anal attack later in the evening. "Hey, that's so unfair," he yelled but they were well gone by that stage. He hurried to the spare bedroom to get himself togged up thinking it would have been just as easy to wear his boutique undies. He stopped dead in his tracks. No wonder they'd wanted him to go searching in there, for naked, propped up on the bed, gagged, tied hand and foot to the bedposts, was Richard. He was struggling to get out of his bondage and failing miserably.

Larry smiled lasciviously, advancing on the poor, hapless victim. Taking pity on him he removed the gag only to be assaulted by a string of abuse.

"Hey," Larry said to calm him, "I had nothing to do with this but if you don't shut the fuck up, I'll stick the gag back in your mouth and leave you here."

That did it. Richard calmed down but not enough that Larry was prepared to loosen the ties. In fact, he quite liked having him at his mercy like that.

"I missed you," Larry said quietly.

Richard laughed but it sounded false in the quiet of the room.

"You don't have to believe me. I don't blame you. I probably handled it all wrong, but of all the guys I was seeing, you were my favorite. Sure, I felt something for all three of you but you were my choice if I could only have one."

"You're a greedy sod, you know that?" Richard retorted. "One should be enough for any man."

"Why?"

Richard spluttered a little, stammered out a few words, but the best he could come up with was, "Because that's the way it's supposed to be."

"When you get back to the city, I'd be delighted if you could show me where that's written."

"Cynical bastard," Richard spat, though his mood seemed to thaw. "You still fucking around with those other two?"

"Yeah, but not as frequently. They've got feelings for each other. They're going to set up house together. Like I hoped you might with me."

Richard seemed genuinely surprised. "What?"

"I was going to ask you to move in with me if we'd been able to work it all out. But you went off in a huff."

"I thought you were just using me."

"I suppose in a way I was. For that I'm sorry. I was developing real feelings for you."

"Me, too. That's why I ran."

"Silly bugger." Larry had been caressing Richard's naked thigh as they spoke and it was obvious now how much Richard cared.

Larry shucked off his clothes and lay on the bed to engulf Richard's straining cock in his mouth.

"I like you a lot, Larry," Richard moaned.

Larry didn't want to take his mouth off the man he'd craved for the past few weeks, even to acknowledge his feelings. He'd let the beautiful man tied to the bed know in his own time.

Neither of them heard the bedroom door close quietly or the whispers as Cary and Tom tiptoed out of the cabin. They'd returned to ensure everything had panned out as they'd planned.

"I think Larry likes his Christmas present," Tom whispered.

"Not as much as Richard likes being the gift," Cary added.

Love and the Odor of Red Leatherette

There I was face down in the back seat of the car, inhaling the odor of red leatherette as my ass was inhaling pounding cock. Did I have no pride? Leatherette, for fuck's sake. Not even real leather. And red? Whose idea of good automobile design was this? And the guy fucking me was overweight and in his forties! Ancient! He was fucking me so aggressively that he was threatening to give my face a good dose of leatherette burn.

No, I had no pride when it came to cock. I was new to the game. And like all converts to a new religion, I was embracing it with open arms, and open ass, and open mouth. It was 1964. I was as ignorant of the world's myriad dark sexual alleyways as any man whose concentration on the freeways of life left him little or no time to take the beckoning detours that would add color and meaning to his journey. But courtesy of the school library dictionary, I did know that I was never going to marry. That was my definition of 'homosexual', at any rate. A well-meaning, unmarried family friend had suggested, in whispers that reeked of intrigue, "Look the word up."

My pocket dictionary had no such listing. Nor did my parent's leather-bound, century-old lexographic heirloom that took pride of place at the bottom of the bookcase. I chanced the school library and was amply rewarded.

Oh, I had thought, that explains the crushes I had on the sexy college jocks and, in particular, the rugged dark captain of the football team. It also explained why I got hard every time I saw them in the shower after a sweaty game. I knew I was different, I just didn't know how different. They told crude tales about girls. I wrote science fiction stories about the close mateship of boys. In *their* adventures, there were lots of blow jobs, hand jobs, cunt licking, and occasional anal sex. In *my* stories, there was lots of hugging. Not in real life though. The early sixties were a whole other universe when it came to gay life.

With the dictionary revelation, I knew my behavior had a name, but I also knew it was considered an illness. I took my temperature. It was normal. I felt my pulse. Normal. If it was an illness, why did all my vital signs show I was in the pink of health? Even though I felt normal, I knew I couldn't talk to my parents about how I longed to touch my college classmates—just there.

Sadly, it wasn't a classmate pounding my ass. It was a guy old enough to be my dad. Nasty thought. Wash my brain. But what he lacked in looks or body sculpturing he made up for in dick size and technique. Let's face it—if it was something I needed badly, it was an education—in sex.

It wasn't like I could read a book or ask a school counselor, I had to learn on the job. How to kiss men. How to suck cock. How to take cock up the ass. Occasionally, one of the men would like you to lick his asshole. Back then it was called rose leafing. Just as I was called 'poofter' or 'camp.'

Henry, I think he told me his name was Henry, was gripping my waist as he gave one last rut, groaning as if he were in pain. He held his cock inside me, shooting his load, although I didn't feel it, before he collapsed on my back. I started to jerk my own cock because I'd found the men who liked to fuck me in the back seats of cars tended to lose all interest once they'd come. It was rare for one of them to wank me off or suck me.

He pulled out and grabbed an oily rag from the glove box. He thrust it at me. "Here, don't get it on the seat." He patted the leatherette upholstery with more tenderness than he'd shown me.

After I shot my load into the decidedly unromantic rag, wiping my knob clean lest some residual cock drool defile his automobile, he told me, "Wipe your ass. I don't want it leaking everywhere."

There was reason for his concern, not so much the love of his car but the love of his wife, and possibly two or three kids, back at home. Like most of my pickups, he wore a wedding ring. They were always in a hurry after they had completed their part of the transaction and couldn't wait to drop me back "somewhere close" to where the initial meeting had occurred.

I was still too young, too green, to realize just how much I was being used. But it wasn't like I wasn't getting any pleasure out of it. I was. In buckets.

And it was in a bucket seat that I had my transcendental experience.

Although no longer a sexual virgin, I was a virgin in real life experience. I'd been fucked frequently ever since I'd discovered the joys of toilet and sand dune sex while visiting my grandmother one mid-term vacation. Nanna lived in a beach suburb about 50 miles from the city. One side was a lake and the other the ocean. It was in her small coastal town, which experienced a large influx of holidaymakers every summer, I'd discovered that men liked to suck other men's cocks. I had not yet had the opportunity to finesse my skill in that department as most men who picked me up preferred to chow down on me or else screw my collegiate ass.

That had first been done by a married man in the grass beneath a beach windmill on a side road from the town's main thoroughfare. I felt no pain the first time; I'd been experimenting with carrots, so my virginity taker did not believe my confessed lack of experience, thus depriving himself of my undying gratitude and his own extra enjoyment.

I learned the basics of male-to-male sex from crude drawings on the back doors of surf club change sheds and toilets. I also learned these were places of assignation, so I spent as many waking hours in or around such places as I could without arousing suspicion. Fortunately, the most thriving of beats was in a park in the town's main road, with a small picnic shelter at which I would sit pretending to read a book after the old men who played chess there vacated for the more disreputable denizens of the night.

Inquisitive men would often come to sit at the next concrete table, eventually plucking up the courage to ask me what I was reading. This inevitably turned into a dreary ass-numbing exercise until they were sure I was 'sympathetic,' then it became an ass-stretching exercise when they drove me to secluded bush areas, poking and prodding for my now non-existent virginity. Not one of the interlopers ever really wanted to know about my literary tastes for real.

Col was one such. He attempted vainly to keep up a conversation about a book and an author he had obviously never heard of as I was heavily into science fiction back then. Eventually, he gave up all pretense, asking if I'd like to go for a drive. It was late afternoon, getting dark quickly, and I knew I would have to be home in a few hours. Col was the best offer I'd had all day. He was late 30s/early 40s, slightly chubby, with a good head of dark hair, and a fairly nondescript appearance. Mr. Average. I couldn't afford to be fussy. Okay, I was slim, blond, and not bad looking, but I was no traffic stopper like the football captain and his team.

As we walked to his car, I told him I would have to be back at this spot within two hours. He assured me that would not be a problem. We drove out past the scrubby aerodrome from which mosquito-sized planes took off for joy flights over the area. I remembered my one and only experience parked near its dark runway one night. I couldn't believe my luck. A very attractive man in his late 20s sat telling me that all it required for him to come was for someone to rub Vaseline on his asshole.

I think I said something like, "That's nice," while waiting impatiently for him to jump me.

"Yea, rub it on my asshole. I just go wild."

Why was this guy so preoccupied with telling me about how excited he gets when lube was plied on his shithole? He must have given me twenty variations of the theme while I sat there waiting to get to the point, which was him slamming his dick in *my* ass! If he'd been more upfront about his requirements it would not have taken me another two years before I sank my cock in someone's butt. I just assumed that if you were the young guy you were the one who got fucked. Which was fine by me. I enjoyed it.

Col kept driving, by this time we were reaching the outer limits of the area in which it would be possible for me to walk home. While I wasn't worried I did ask where we were going.

He told me, "Somewhere really safe."

It made sense because his car was a Volkswagen Beetle. Too small for backseat fucking. He was obviously looking for somewhere safe in the open air. It did become tedious after a while though, having to keep up small talk as neither of us was really interested in what the other had to say; all we wanted was sex. My main concern was that the longer he drove, taking into account the time needed to be doubled in order to get back, the less time there was for the actual deed.

Finally, we turned off on to a dirt road. Col cut the lights as we crawled up the steep incline, the sound of the car setting off the dogs in the houses clinging to the base of the hill. As we rose higher, it became bush land and, once at the top, a dead end, Col turned the car so it looked straight back down the hill. It was eerily quiet and dark apart from watery, uninquisitive moonlight. It was the perfect vantage point to watch for anyone approaching.

Obviously, Col had used this lover's lane before, but I thought it prudent not to ask for confirmation. We waited to see if the dogs barking had elicited any curiosity, but no one emerged from their home so Col leaned over, pulling me toward him. He kissed me. About half the guys kissed. I didn't like it much. They attempted to stick their tongues down my throat. They tasted of cigarettes or beer. Or desperation. The others made no pretense that our coupling was any more than it was; a quick release for them, another notch in my sexual education for me.

But Col was different. His mouth was clean as minty toothpaste, his tongue didn't stab, and his mouth didn't vacuum pump my tongue until it was sore at the root. He was gentle and encouraging; it was the first time I enjoyed swapping saliva and running my tongue across another person's tonsils.

I thought this would be a preliminary to getting out of the car for the main event, especially after he opened the car doors. The interior light cast a feeble blue glow allowing him to really look at me, "You really are a good looking kid." Right then I would have done anything for this man.

He helped me remove my clothes. I always wore T-shirts and loose jeans, all the better to get in and out of quickly. He pulled his shirt over his head as I ran my fingers through the hairs on his belly. He let me unbuckle him, and pull down the zip on his trousers, before he shucked them and his underpants down to his ankles. I moved aside so he could take them off completely, but he just leaned across to the glove box to take out a jar of lubrication.

"Here, straddle me," he said. I faced him, easing my knees on either side of his legs. I leaned in to kiss him again. While I did, he began to massage my asshole with the grease. It felt good, him swishing it around my butthole with his finger, every now and then pushing it in a little way to loosen me up. I wasn't used to this sort of consideration. Often it was a gob of spit on my asshole and a fist of spit on his cock, and wham!

Col's digital penetrations were making me hard so he smeared a little grease on my cock, giving it a few jerks. I stopped him. I was so excited I knew I'd come too quickly. He understood and went back to penetrating my more-than-receptive ass. Once he had two fingers inside me, I was panting my excitement. He told me to squat over his cock and lower my butt.

It was cramped, uncomfortable, but he'd moved to the passenger's seat so I didn't have to worry about the steering wheel or inadvertently honking the horn. I felt him position his cock at the entrance to my ass.

"Slide down slowly," he said.

I eased myself down, feeling his cock breach my guts. My sharp intake of breath made him stop for a while until I relaxed. Then my body sank further, opening up for him. I paused again but within moments, I wanted more. I moved my body upwards, clenching my sphincter so that it grasped his prick and suctioned it tightly as I rose, then I sank down to his balls. He was average size, but I had never had a cock embedded so far inside me. This was a new position, and I liked it.

He encouraged me to continue milking his cock in this way, every now and then pushing up hard to meet my descending stroke until I thought his prick would break through into my stomach. I forced my body down onto his cock harder and harder until he was so far inside me my balls were roiling. He kissed me hard, and then broke the lip lock to stare at me so intensely I got embarrassed. It was as if he saw something familiar in my face. He held me to him closely but tenderly as he took over the action. He pistoned his cock up my ass as my own rubbed against his belly.

He whispered, "I love you."

Don't be stupid, I thought. *He's making believe I'm his wife.*

"I love you," he said again as he pushed his cock into my guts.

Once I could understand. But he said it twice. There was no use in pointing out how foolish he'd been to tell another male that he loved him. Love was for men and women. What two men had going for them was sex. I didn't want to spoil the mood so I let it go, concentrating on my orgasm that was building through no manipulation on my part. His cock was massaging something inside me that I'd never felt before, making me ready to shoot.

I warned him. "Um…I think I'm gonna come soon."

He panted. "Me, too."

I was waiting for him to give me the usual rag, plus the lecture about not getting it on the upholstery. Instead, he merely kissed me again, then held me so tight he pushed my face into the top of the leatherette seat where I could smell the residue of hair oil and countless other sex trysts. It was a heady odor. His pounding was giving me such intense pleasure I started spewing jizz onto his chest. The contractions in my asshole set him off. "Oh, yeah. Oh, yeah. That's it. Oh, yeah. Oh, I fuckin' love you."

I collapsed, the full length of his cock embedded inside me until it began to shrink and eventually popped out. He leaned over to the glove box to fetch a hand towel, wiping the goop that had adhered to our stomachs and chests, before he slowly lifted me to wipe my ass. As I usually took care of that myself, I must have blushed because he handed me the towel, looking away while I did it. Then he wiped the spooge from his dick and balls.

We dressed in silence. As I slipped on my T-shirt, he started the car, and I slammed the door closed as he took off down the hill, this time with his headlights on.

On the drive back he kept glancing sideways at me. "How long you been doing this sort of thing?"

"Not long."

"You gotta be careful. There are guys out there who want to hurt young guys like you."

"You sound like my mum," I said.

He was startled. "Your mum knows you do this?"

"Hell, no. She just warned me not to get into cars with strange men because they'll cut my dick off."

He laughed. "Now you know what they really want to do with your dick."

We drove on in silence.

"You know back there?" I hesitated.

He tensed. "What about it?"

"You remember what you said?"

"I think so. What part of it?"

I was getting uncomfortable. "You know."

"No, I don't." He looked worried now.

"That bit where you said you love me."

"Oh, that?"

"Yeah."

"Did that embarrass you?" he asked.

"Not exactly."

"What then?"

"Well, two men can't love each other. Not like a man and a woman."

He smiled. "Can't they?"

"No." I was adamant.

"You don't want to believe everything you read in books. Or what your parents tell you. Or even teachers and psychologists, for that matter."

"They can then?"

He looked over at me to check I was for real. "What? Love each other?" I nodded. "Sure, they can. Don't you go gooey in the stomach sometimes when you see a guy you like?"

I did.

"Aren't there men you dream about being with? About wanking with? Guys your age you can't get out of your mind."

"Like the football captain, you mean?"

"Is he good looking?"

"Uh huh."

"You think about him a lot?"

"Yeah," I admitted.

"That's a sort of love."

"Wow."

"And when you get older you'll fall in love with a girl and get married and ..."

"No, I won't. I'm camp."

"Well, in that case you'll fall in love with a man and set up a home together."

"You mean there are men who live together like a husband and wife?"

"Yes. Lots of them. But they have to keep it very quiet because it's against the law."

"Stupid law!"

"Yeah."

"Young guys, not just old guys?"

"All ages."

I sat quietly for a long time.

"And you think that could happen to me?"

"Definitely," he said. "You're one good looking kid. Who wouldn't want to settle down with you one day?"

"Would you?"

"Would I what?"

"Settle down with me?"

He sighed. "I would love to. More than anything. But I made my choice, and I'm stuck with it."

We were back at the pick-up spot, but before I got out of his cozy Volkswagen, again with blood-red leatherette seats—car interiors, like my men, were beginning to take on a monotonous sameness—he held my hand for a moment as if he wanted to tell me something important, then he let me go. I got out of the car. We'd been gone five minutes shy of the two hours.

As he drove off, he rolled down the window. "Hey, kid! Make the right choice for you. And have a great life."

My life would never be the same after that meeting. Col would never know what he had done for me. I had some very serious thinking to do. A total reappraisal of where I thought my life was going. Sex would never just be sex again. There was the chance of...well, I couldn't think about that right now. All ages, he'd said. Hmmm.

The world was suddenly full of possibilities. And they didn't involve red leatherette.

It's All Greek to Me

Nothing much had changed in six years. The taverna where the young men of the village lazed away the afternoon and evening may have received a coat of paint and whitewash since that time although it looked remarkably as I remembered it, just not as noisy, not as bustling, not as overwhelming. But then, the last time I'd been here I was a naïve fourteen-year-old bleeding from a head wound, unconscious of my surroundings as I'd been carried to the ferry and on to the mainland hospital.

There was nothing to say things had remained the same although six years is not long in Greek village terms, although it's a lifetime to a teenager.

I was being ridiculous. Not an unusual behavioral pattern for me. I'd traveled half way around the world for a fantasy. People have probably done more in pursuit of their dreams and ambitions but I was predicating mine on an act of kindness, something so flimsy that if I stopped to think about it, I would more than likely turn around and head straight back home. So I was doing everything in my power not to think about it. And failing miserably.

The bus that met the early morning ferry – it may have been the same bus that picked me up last time it was so familiar – dropped me off in the central square with my backpack and my seriously high hopes; the sum total of the baggage I'd brought with me. It all looked smaller somehow, not just because I was now an adult rather than a child and with age comes perspective, but more as if the village had flinched and drawn in on itself for protection against the economic woes that wracked the country.

I had always taken Greece for granted when I was younger. My family came here every year for the summer holidays because my father loved the place and because he was blessed with a lack of imagination. He would not even contemplate a change to his schedule. His attitude was that if you liked something there was no need to change it. If my mother attempted to inject variety into our day-to-day living, my father would fly into a rage for days on end. He was not of a curious bent and was surprised that I turned out to be.

He, my mother and myself stayed in the same hotel every summer and if he didn't get the same room it put him quite out of temper for the first few days and, at the end of our time there he would lecture the manager on the absolute necessity of allocating us Room 316 each and every year, not because it had the best views of the coast or of the courtyard, it didn't, but because it was familiar.

My father was a formal man; I always referred to him as father. It never occurred to me to think of him as dad. A university professor in Greek art and history, he passed on his love of things classical to me. It was his one passion and the only time I saw him become animated. That, and what happened the year I turned fourteen.

I did not inherit my father's caution, I was more free spirited like my mum who had dampened her natural enthusiasm in order to suit my father's pace and style. She would always sigh softly as the bus deposited us in the same square each year with the same luggage. She would glance about trying to notice any changes that might have occurred in the twelve months since we were last here. I doubt she ever found any either.

On my own this time, I made my way to the same hotel even though I could afford better, with more up-to-date facilities, better staff, panoramic views, but I was not here for a holiday, this was more a pilgrimage.

As I passed the tavernes, their chairs upturned waiting for the waiters to upend them before the locals arrived to take their places for the passing parade of sightseers from the mainland or the tourists who spent longer periods here to laze on the sandy beach below the cliff face. The beach was one of the reasons for the island's popularity but the difficulty in reaching it also meant the island would never be one of the 'hot spots' like the more amenable Santorini or Mykonos. It required real effort to trek to the sandy shoreline so only the really committed, the fit, came here. It was an acquired taste, but a taste, however, that became less acquired and more popular as travel guides, ever eager in their search for something new, began to promote it for its quieter 'lifestyle,' an alternative to the younger sex-crazed mob mentality of the big name resorts.

But the island, and its quaint villages, was known by the cognoscenti for something else: the local men. I'm sure my father had no idea of its reputation when he chose it for our annual vacation, basing his selection purely on availability, quiet, and its singular lack of major archeological attractions that would have ramped up the tourist traffic, so he could spend his time re-reading his Greek texts, luxuriating in his specialist's knowledge of the country. That left me free to clamber over ancient stone structures that made no sense to me except as playthings.

I did wonder in later life if my father might have harbored secret longings which he indulged via voyeurism at the local male population, but I could think of no indication he gave of that, nor do I believe he harbored any feelings in that direction. I think he was just happy to be here. Eventually my mother would cease her sighs and fall in step with my father. They left me to my own devices, a freedom I seldom earned back home.

I had become friendly with a few of the local lads because they saw my face every year and they allowed me to join their games on the beach. They had a smattering of English, and I had a smattering of Greek, but as puberty hit they stopped their games to concentrate on the women who arrived, alone, aching for companionship and were not above paying for it. That, after all, was the island's unofficial main source of income. Sex tourism was its covert lifeblood.

I would have taken it as an omen had I been allocated the same room my father insisted on year after year, but I wasn't. There were so few guests this late in the season that my room did overlook the sea from a balcony so tiny it comfortably sat just two with barely enough room for a small table for drinks and snacks. The other side overlooked the plateia but the window was shaded with heavy curtains in case the occupant was disturbed by the tavernes and their al fresco seating that remained open late into the night, though I doubted a mere curtain would block the sounds of pealing laughter, the clink of glasses, or the loud conversations of men.

It would be another hour before the tavernes opened at noon so I lay on the bed to rest, my heart thumping in expectation, my much more practical mind preparing me for disappointment. My head throbbed, heralding one of those awful migraines that had plagued me for years. If I didn't do something now, I would be incapacitated for days. The pills were in the front pocket of my rucksack but I was too lethargic, so overcome by the enormity of my stupidity, my body refused to move. Perhaps it was a safety mechanism.

The headaches began that last year we visited. I didn't draw the same conclusion that my father did; that what occurred that fateful day was responsible for everything that happened subsequently. That somehow Greece had turned me gay. For the rest of his life he blamed himself. He died three short years later, I suspect from disappointment, puzzled that life changes, that people change, including his own son. I wished I could speak to him and tell him that far from ruining my life it had set me free. I believed in that, regardless of the outcome, good or bad, of this return visit.

My mother, more grief stricken than I would ever have imagined at his death, nevertheless married again after a suitable period of mourning. This time to a man full of life and inquisitiveness, the antithesis of my father, but she soon bored of him, divorcing him eighteen months after their marriage, referring to her liaison as 'a mistake.'

"After your father I thought it was what I wanted, but it wasn't," she said simply.

She eventually found the life she sought living alone but surrounded by a group of supportive friends of the same mind. She never lacked for company, for friends with whom to visit the galleries, restaurants, shows she had a mind to visit while leaving her with enough time to spend quietly, alone.

It was she who encouraged me to return to Greece. "Even if nothing comes of it, Tommy, you will have tried. It's important to try."

My father had left everything to my mother apart from a small but generous allowance that allowed me an independence that would otherwise have been beyond my reach. I did inherit my father's cautious nature concerning things financial so I invested wisely and even during the worst of the world's economic woes, I was little affected. Caution may not lead to vast increases in wealth but it does firewall you from vast sudden decreases when things go bad.

The sound of activity: laughter, raised voices, the clink of glasses, the scrape of chairs woke me. I kept my eyes closed because the headache reacted badly to light. I needed to get to my pills, regretting now that I had not taken one earlier. I stumbled out of bed, feeling my way gingerly to where I thought I'd left my bag, knocking into the heavy wooden furniture but somehow managing to avoid damage to my toes. In the end, I had to cover my eyes and peek between my fingers to locate my backpack because everything was so unfamiliar.

I braced for the pain between my eyes. It didn't come. My response had been so automatic after all these years that I'd failed to notice I did not have a migraine at all. Looking at my watch, I discovered I had slept for hours exhausted no doubt from the long distance I had flown.

Tension, however, knotted my body and would do so until I made the first move. The shower did little to relax me, but I felt calmer and fresher for bathing. I changed my clothes to those items that showed me to my best advantage. If I was going to advertise, nothing says 'good breeding' better than designer labels. It was the bait to snare my prey.

I had deliberately avoided looking from my window at the tavernes around the plateia, nervous lest I chicken out and catch the first ferry back to the mainland, and then go home. Except I had no real home, no real roots. My mother had carved out a niche for herself into which she settled comfortably. I had yet to find mine but I was young, there was plenty of time.

I opened the door to my room, shaking as I took the first steps into the unknown. I felt a little like the heroines of those novels by E.M. Forster and others who find themselves freed of their tight little lives by the exotic warmer climes of the Mediterranean. What was my excuse? I came from a climate that was as similar to Greece's as the olive oil in my kitchen.

Downstairs in the small lobby, I greeted the young women behind the counter who went from bored ennui to garrulous in the blink of an eye. It was obviously because I was young, foreign, and dressed in label clothes. The inhabitants of the island could pick those visitors worth cultivating at a hundred paces.

I was polite and friendly; she might come in handy for information later on. I allowed her to recommend a few spots to visit before thanking her profusely and tipping her extravagantly. It was patronizing and I hated doing it, but I hadn't come here to fail.

Out in the bright sunlight, I glanced around the various tavernes dotting the area and my eyes honed in on him. I stumbled on the uneven stone of the town square because I had not expected to see him on my first outing. It may have been six years but there was no mistaking him, even if I hadn't seen the distinctive astrology tattoo on his chest above his nipple. He wore tight jeans and a shirt open to the waist to reveal his tanned torso and the ripped muscles that were so attractive to foreigners. If anything, maturity had added a certain luster to his looks so that he was so sexually alluring it quite threw me. If I'd had a gun I would have shot that smug, self-satisfied prick to hell.

It hadn't occurred to me that he would be here as well. Stupid of me. If the man I sought was here, then surely my nemesis would be as well. Perching my sun glasses on my nose and taking a deep breath for courage I made my way toward the tables in the shade of the taverna's striped canvas awning. I knew the men at the adjacent table, all locals, were watching me without giving any indication they were doing so. They were appraising me. Friend or foe? Troublemaker? Someone they could make money from? At times like this, I would have given anything to be able to read minds.

As I passed their table I lifted my sun glasses to the top of my head, ran my eyes over them, smiled, and wished them a good morning in English, even though I speak fluent Greek. I glanced around, as if undecided, before seating myself a few tables behind them, and ordered a light snack with coffee from the owner who appeared after one of the young men called to him that he had a customer.

I'd seen the look of consternation on Nikos's face, as if he recognized me but couldn't find me in his bank of memories. That was because the last time he had seen me I was a young teenager, covered in blood.

I eavesdropped on the men's conversation, watching them surreptitiously above the pages of the week old English-language newspaper I was pretending to read, folding it away when my coffee arrived. They had spent scant little breath discussing me except to wonder at the likelihood of my being on the prowl for cunt. One of them suggested it was boy cunt I was after.

"Loukas will find out," one of them said.

At the sound of his name, I looked up, straight into the eyes of the smiling Nikos. It unnerved me. Not the smile or that he was examining me like some sort of specimen under a microscope, but that Loukas was the man I had come looking for. It was confirmation he was still around. A few minutes later, Nikos took leave of his friends and my hope was he had gone in search of Loukas to tell him of the familiar stranger in town, one whose interest peaked at the mention of his name.

Even though I waited through another coffee and a beer, neither man appeared. I paid my bill, gathered my few possessions together, to head off on my first and what promised to be my most traumatic pilgrimage. There were a lot of trails leading from the edge of the town, walks along the cliff tops to the forlorn Greco-Roman ruins, or shortcuts across country to neighboring villages. My feet automatically took the weathered path toward the beach that was the town's glory.

The path was steep, made even more precarious by the pebbles spread to stop erosion from the constant foot traffic, and now slippery from the sea spray. I was unafraid as I had made this journey countless times before and never stumbled although I found I was not as agile as I had been as an adventurous 14-year-old. My mind wandered for a moment and I lost my footing, tumbling ass over tit down the path until the edge of the steep incline loomed ahead.

It was not a sheer drop onto rocks below but a fall would have serious consequences, a slide through skin scraping bushes with prickles that would cut and rocks that would bruise as a body hurtled to the beach below unless you managed to grab hold of some sort of support on your downward trajectory.

I grabbed at anything I thought might stop my journey but it all came away in my hand. I gave a little prayer to all the Greek gods I could think of in preparation for the worst, closed my eyes in a futile effort to protect them, and felt my body tilt. I also felt a strong grip on my arm and I found myself suspended off the side of the path, almost certain injury below me.

Levering myself up as best I could, dislodging stones and soil attempting to get a foothold, I was yanked ungraciously back to safety. Lying on the pebbles to get my breath back, waiting for my heart to stop beating fit to burst, and for the adrenaline to cease pumping, I gazed up at my benefactor.

Wouldn't you know my luck? It was Nikos. I laughed, probably more hysterically at my good fortune than at the humor of the situation. For a second it crossed my mind that if I kicked out I could easily topple Nikos over the side to cuts and abrasions or, hopefully, broken limbs. What was the point? He would not understand why I did it.

He offered me his hand, hoisting me to my feet and pulling me against his body. The skin on his chest was smooth and warm, the sweat running in rivulets between his impressive pecs. I wanted to run my fingers across his tattoo, lean my head against him and…and what?

My mind was a jumble of emotions and for the first time since my arrival in Greece, I realized my feelings were raw, wound up like a spring watch ready to snap at the least provocation. My fall was a timely warning.

"Thank you," I panted, falling easily into speaking Greek. "You saved my life."

He brushed off my gratitude. "I don't think so. A few bruises perhaps but death is not so easy."

"Nevertheless, I'm extremely grateful. You must allow me to…"

It was galling to be beholden to a man I detested, but he had still saved me from injury. I owed him that much.

"No," he said sharply, and then added in a milder tone. "No, you owe me nothing."

I knew that was a tourist scam. Humbly reject the first offer. The whole process ends with you rewarding them double.

"Are you going to the beach?" he inquired.

"Yes, perhaps you could guide me down if you're going that way."

During our descent, we swapped small talk. I discovered he had remained on the island to care for his terminally ill mother who had died a little under a year ago from cancer, his dad having drowned at sea a decade before. He was the family breadwinner from that time, unable and unwilling to join the exodus fleeing to the mainland and points north in the Eurozone to improve his lot. Now that his mother had died, he had no reason to stay. All over Europe, small towns and villages lost their young folk to the bright lights and better economic future of the major cities. He had no curiosity about me, almost as if he knew why I was there, although that was impossible.

It's not a good idea to learn enough about your enemy that it humanizes him and I regretted I had to consciously maintain my hatred of Nikos because I was in danger of liking the guy. What's not to like? He was good looking enough to turn heads, his body buff and beautiful, the ink on his chest just adding to its desirability, and he had an easy charm that was as seductive as sweet honey. This guy must have women lining up around the block.

Yes, I knew gay men would find him incredibly beddable but I also knew what he thought of gay men. I'd learned it first-hand.

When we reached the beach, we both removed our footwear, the sand crunching between our toes. I headed off toward my ultimate goal while he tagged along without saying a word. The closer we got to the boulders on the rocky point the more my revulsion at the man beside me stirred until, by the time I hoisted myself onto the top of one of the most prominent outcrops, I was almost ready to push him off as he clambered up beside me.

We sat in silence. From the corner of my eye, I could see him staring at me as I seethed. I didn't have the words to tell him how much I detested him, so I sat mute as the poison ate away at me like it had for the past six years.

It must have been about ten minutes before either of us spoke, and it was he who broke the silence.

"This was where I hurt you," he said quietly.

I looked over, surprised.

"You know who I am?"

"I recognized you the moment you appeared at the taverna, Tommy" he said. "I have never forgotten you."

"For six years I have wanted to kill you, Nikos," I said calmly.

"And now?"

"I want to hurt you so bad."

He said nothing but reached over to pick up a large rock, handing it to me without comment. I wanted to smash his handsomeness to hell and back and he deserved no less, or crush his hand that was spread enticingly close. In the end I smacked the rock into the side of his head and left him there, unconscious and bleeding, before I made my way back to the hotel.

Did I feel any satisfaction in what I'd done? Fuck, yeah! It was an unexpected bonus to my trip. I was so pleased with myself, so elated by my good fortune, I lay down for a nap, the heat and the sun so debilitating that I needed a mid-afternoon siesta.

I may have been satisfied with my revenge but my mind wasn't. It was in turmoil. That smack on the side of his head did not make up for the six years of pain, or the upheaval in my life, for my family never returned to Greece after that fateful summer. The sound from outside the hotel, the shouts and yells from the plateia blurred into the shouts and laughter on the beach, the one I visited that afternoon six years before. My younger self was running around with a mob of the local boys all roughly his own age. He looked down at his youthful, slightly overfed privileged body which stood out against the wiry muscles of the locals.

They were engaged in a game of beach football watched indulgently by the older local boys in their twenties. One, in particular, had taken his fancy although he would be hard put to define his feelings. All he knew was that Loukas, stripped to his shorts, his olive skin glistening with sweat and sea water, invaded his dreams at night. He wanted more than anything to see Loukas naked, to be held in his arms. He felt his own little stiffy tent in his bathers.

He also felt the ball as it hit him square in the face, bloodying his nose. He'd dropped his concentration, distracted by his close proximity to Loukas, and hadn't seen the ball coming. It knocked him on his ass, the opposing team laughing at his humiliation pointing at his cock which stubbornly refused to go down. His own team cursed him for his stupidity. Someone must have noticed his preoccupation with Loukas because they called out 'poustis.' Faggot.

Young Tommy was only too aware what it meant and what the accusation would do to his fragile friendships on the island. Both teams took up the chant, some of the older men joining the chorus. His hero Loukas looked embarrassed. That was enough to reduce Tommy to tears. The boys threw sand and soda cans at him, all the time calling him 'faggot.' The sand got in his eyes and his mouth as he ran away from the abuse, the cans and stones hurting less than the accusations. He ran and ran until he got a stitch and had to sit down for fear of throwing up. He had never felt so miserable in his life.

He heard Loukas shout at the boys to stop it, that it was not the Greek way to treat a visitor with such disrespect. His hero took the time to walk over to where he sat to brush the sand out of his eyes and wipe his nose, running with snot and humiliation. Loukas told him only babies cried and that everything would be better tomorrow, that he should go back to the hotel but not tell his parents anything about what had happened.

He did as Loukas told him, turning up on the beach the next day as if nothing had changed. But it had. The boys who had been his friends shut him out of their games. They turned their backs on him. Loukas didn't notice because he was more interested in the older female tourists who flooded the island this time of the year. It was not something he could discuss with his parents, they would just do what they always did, look embarrassed and tell him he was too young.

Too young for what?

For the remainder of his stay, Tommy took long solitary walks, careful to be away from the hotel in case his father asked why he was not playing with his little Greek friends. Sometimes he stalked Loukas just to be near him, not understanding the funny feelings he got in his belly when Loukas was around. It was all so new to him. Much later he would recognize the feelings for what they were, but at fourteen the world of emotions, of sexual feelings, was as foreign as an explanation of puberty from his father.

It was on such a day, a day he was shadowing his hero that the worst happened. He had seen Loukas disappear often enough with women but on this occasion he was with an older man, of around fifty, wending his way down onto the beach. The day was blustery, the wind whipping up the sand so that it stung as it swirled around his ankles. The beach was deserted. Keeping in amongst the scrubby myrtle and oleander bushes, he followed the two men, watching as they ran along the beach toward the rocks.

When they disappeared, he dared to venture forth hugging the cliff face, reaching the outcrop without discovery. He heard whispered voices from between the boulders so he inched his way up the tallest of the rocks in order to survey his surroundings.

At first, he couldn't really make out what the two men were doing, although he could see they were naked. Loukas was on his knees, the older man's cock in his mouth. Tommy had no concept of oral sex so he was puzzled and fascinated at the same time. Eventually, Loukas stood and bent over one of the smaller stones, parting his ass cheeks. The man had a tube of sunscreen and squirted some on his fingers rubbing it into Loukas's hole before greasing his own cock. He pushed it into Loukas who grunted like he was in pain. Still the older man pushed until he was right against Loukas's back, the two of them sweating from the effort.

The older man began what Tommy knew adults called fucking because he had heard bigger boys at school talking about it. Up until now, he thought it was something only men and women did to each other. His little cock was hard as it had ever been because he realized, without knowing why, this is what he wanted to do with Loukas himself...

He slipped his hand into his shorts to play with his prick hoping that one day it would grow to the size of Loukas's. The older man made a lot of animal sounds telling Loukas he was about to come in his ass. Boy, there was a lot they left out of sex lessons at school. Tommy thought maybe he should go to the headmaster when he returned and explain that Mr. Peterson, his Sex Ed instructor, was only giving the class half the story.

Their coupling complete, the older man pulled out and sank to his knees as Loukas turned to lean back against the rock, his cock standing out proudly from his body. The man put his mouth over it and Loukas leaned his head back in pleasure. The moment before he closed his eyes, he saw Tommy above him, watching. His face broke into a smile and he winked, and then he closed his eyes to surrender to the pleasure. A few minutes later, he held the back of the man's head, swore a few times and it all seemed to be over.

Loukas looked to see if Tommy was still there, mouthing silently to 'fuck off' but smiling as he said so. Tommy nodded and skidded from view but he wanted to see what they did next. Sneaking a look over the rim of the rock, he noticed that the older man had retrieved his wallet now that he was dressed and counted out a large amount of cash into Loukas's hand.

"Worth every penny," the older man said.

"If you want a repeat," Loukas encouraged.

"Don't you worry about that," the older man replied. "I'm here until the end of the week."

Loukas folded the money and put it in his back pocket. "You know where to find me."

Tommy kept his head down as the two men emerged from their hiding place heading toward the path back to town. His education had broadened tremendously in one afternoon.

A loud voice startled all three of them. He'd been sprung. Nikos, his face a blaze of fury, spat out the cursed word 'Poustis,' over and over until Tommy cringed under the onslaught. Too late he saw the stone in Nikos's hand, the impact of it knocking him off his rock perch, splitting open the side of his head. He fell onto the sand bloodied, only half conscious, taking little notice of the shouts and curses that rent the air.

From what he pieced together later, he gathered that the older man quickly escaped the scene of the assault, encouraged to do so by Loukas who turned on his friend. He heard the accusations of 'faggot' bandied about again but he was beyond caring. He remembered Nikos gazing into his eyes but he could scarcely focus. Nikos said something but Tommy couldn't make it out. Then Nikos ran.

Loukas attempted to clean the wound, obviously hoping that it was superficial enough that Tommy would be able to pass it off as a fall, but the bleeding wouldn't stop. Lifting him into his arms, Loukas walked quickly across the sand, speaking calmly, reassuring him that everything would be all right. Tommy believed him because he felt so protected. Loukas told him he should not ever tell his parents or anyone else what he'd witnessed because they would not understand and it would get them all into awful trouble. If they asked how he got his injury, he should say he slipped on the rocks and banged his head.

To the best of his ability, because he was almost incoherent, Tommy said he would. In return, Loukas kissed him on the lips, telling him if he was a good boy one day he would do for him what he'd done for the older man. Tommy swore it would be their secret before he felt Loukas running, running as if his life depended on it.

He remembered voices and shouting and his mum crying but nothing really until he woke up in a hospital bed in Athens. Apart from the headache, he felt fine and eagerly asked when they were going back to the hotel to continue their holiday. When they told him they were going home, he begged, he pleaded, he cried to be taken back to the island, but nothing worked. They left Greece a few days later and as a family, they never returned.

The sound of cheers in the square interrupted my dream of the past. I staggered bleary eyed to the window, smiling when I saw Nikos's audacity. He was seated at a table in the taverna, a tell-tale patch against the side of his head. Obviously, I hadn't hit him nearly hard enough. But the loud fuss wasn't over Nikos, it was because of an individual who had turned up with a fistful of cash. The breath caught in my throat as I watched Loukas order drinks for his cronies.

He was as magnificent as I remembered, but how to approach him? I couldn't just bowl up to the man and say "You owe me. I kept my side of the bargain, now you keep yours." Not six years after the event. Loukas obviously never expected to have to pay out. He wouldn't even remember me, let alone our pact.

The noise subsided as the waiter brought out the drinks. Loukas and Nikos were deep in conversation, glancing up at my window several times although I was standing far enough back in the dark that they would not see me. They seemed to being arguing until, finally, Loukas impatiently broke away, striding purposefully across the square toward the hotel.

I was trembling; he didn't look at all pleased.

Five minutes passed before there was a quiet knock at my room. For a split second, I contemplated not answering but desire overcame my reluctance and I flung open the door. Loukas smiled but not quickly enough to disguise the look that revealed he had no idea who I was. How could he forget and Nikos remember?

"Hey," he said.

I stepped aside and invited him in. I'll admit he lied beautifully. "Long time, no see."

"You don't remember me, do you?"

He held up his hand in protest. "Of course I do. It's so good to see you after, what is it, six years?"

Nikos had obviously coached him well.

"Yes, six long years," I agreed.

Suddenly I was in his arms, his tongue wedged in my mouth, but it was all technique and little passion. "I've missed you so much, Bobby," he said. Obviously Nikos's coaching only went so far, but I didn't bother to correct him.

Perhaps it was my fault for expecting too much and things would get better as we overcame our initial embarrassment.

"I knew you'd come back," he whispered. For a moment I believed him.

He undressed me easily as I put up no resistance, shucking off his own clothes with a speed that showed he was well practiced. It gave me a chance to admire him, his body still in great shape although it was certainly not as buff as Nikos's, he was packing a few extra kilos, just as his eyes weren't the clear pools that Nikos's were, or his pecs and biceps those of a laborer like…shit, how did Nikos get into my head? Loukas picked me up in his powerful arms, smothering me with his kisses which finally began to convince my body of his sincerity. My cock hardened as he lay me down on the bed climbing in beside me in such a way that he could push his cock into my mouth.

I would have preferred if he'd slowed the pace a little, it was going much too fast considering I'd waited six years. Maybe he was just over-keen. It was churlish of me to complain now that I was getting precisely what I wanted. Okay, not precisely.

My fantasy was way more romantic. Reality, unfortunately, had a way of intruding. When I took his cock into my mouth the taste almost made me gag. He'd obviously already had sex today because I tasted traces of pussy and shit on his cock. The idea excited me somehow and over-ruled the part of my brain that told me I was being duped. Had I expected him to remain chaste for six years? He had no idea I'd ever return. And it's not as if he knew I was in town. No, I'd forgive him.

All too soon, he removed his thick cock from my mouth even as I tried to keep it between my lips, eager to suck him until he came. He must have liked what I was doing because he'd groaned his appreciation. Now he had other ideas and rolled me onto my stomach, propping my ass up with pillows. I don't mind what position I'm in when guys penetrate my ass but for my first time with Loukas I really would have preferred it on my back. All my romantic fantasies were crashing and burning.

He scooted off the bed to retrieve lubrication which he must carry in his pocket for all occasions. I felt a twinge of jealousy but mentally talked myself out of it so as not to spoil this grand occasion. He greased my ass, spreading a liberal amount of the gel on the outside and inside of my butt hole, inserting two fingers to open me up. It felt so good I almost blew my load into the bed. I expected him to add a third finger because his cock was a great deal thicker than I was used to. Again, I was out of luck.

He'd greased his prick, pushing it against the entrance to my bowels. It bloody hurt and not in a good way.

"Take it easy," I croaked.

"You don't like it rough?"

I wondered what sort of people he'd been fucking. "No, I don't like it rough."

"Sorry," he said, withdrawing to lather more lube in my ass, using three fingers this time to loosen me. It felt good and when I murmured my appreciation, he took that as the signal to try again. This time his cock slid slowly into my ass with the minimum of burn. Fuck, he felt good inside me. When he began to thrust, hitting my prostate, I thought he was going to have to scrape me off the wall.

Of course, I'd had sex before, but never like this, although I did wonder if my mind was romanticizing it out of proportion. I didn't care, pushing back against his invading prick, eager to take more. If only he'd stop calling me Bobby as he told me how hot my ass was.

I could live with it – for now. I was in serious danger of blowing a load without even touching myself and I sensed he was close as well. He sped up, panting, praising my technique, closer now —

The screech of a female voice from the square below could have peeled paint off the side of a house. It threw him off his stroke and it made my head ring. Whatever it was, it ruined the mood. Loukas was suddenly jittery, swearing vehemently. The voice continued its tirade and I distinctly heard Loukas's name. The guys in the taverna sounded as if they were attempting to placate her but she was having none of it.

Loukas tried to keep up the pace in my ass but it was a losing battle and in the end, he pulled out, slapped me on the cheeks, and apologized. "Shit, sorry, I gotta go. You know how it is."

No, I didn't know how it was. All I knew was after six years and a trip half way around the world all I'd got out of it was a perfunctory fuck from a man who couldn't even get my name right. Or blow his load.

The harridan kept up her caterwauling as Loukas almost fell over himself in his hurry to get dressed. He ran from the room promising to return as soon as he could.

"I promise," he said as he disappeared down the corridor.

Then why did he look so relieved as if the cavalry had arrived in the nick of time? I gave him the benefit of the doubt. That lasted only as long as it took me to discover my wallet open among my pile of clothes, all the cash, amounting to a couple of hundred euros, removed. Fortunately, the credit cards were intact.

I cursed Loukas, I cursed my own stupidity. I went to the window and watched as he ran into the waiting arms of a woman in clothing twenty years too young for her, skin as parched as leather and hair bleached to within an inch of falling out. Her accent singled her out as a tourist on the trawl for young fresh meat to satisfy her. Loukas obviously fit the bill. He didn't even give my window a second glance as he and his temporary bride made themselves comfortable in the tavern among all the other young men who would benefit from Loukas's special relationship with the rich tourist. Only Nikos looked up at my window, his face, I thought, sad and disappointed.

Flinging myself back on the bed, I determined to leave the foul island in the morning, sneak away on the first ferry, forget I'd ever been here, and write off the previous six years as a young man's foolish fantasy. People are right; you can't go back. I gave in to my raw emotions and heaved a sigh that became sobs. I was feeling sorry for myself. I am so very very stupid, so very very naïve.

I must have been making so much noise I didn't hear anyone enter the room until I felt a weight beside me on the bed, and the tender touch of understanding stroking my hair. For a moment, I thought Loukas had come back but as I lay my head on his chest, I saw the astrological signs. I didn't care that it was Nikos or that he may wish me harm for what I'd done earlier that day.

He let me cry myself to sleep, exhausted from the emotional upheaval I'd gone through in the space of one day. The expected nightmares never eventuated; instead, I basked in the warmth and protection of the body against which I lay, the strong arms around me and the comfort of his feather-light fingers caressing my face.

When I finally awoke the sun had set, the room plunged into semi-shadow but illuminated sufficiently by the lights of the surrounding tavernes for me to see that I was not alone on the bed. Somewhere during my exhausted sleep, Nikos had slipped off his clothes and now sprawled naked on the bed beside me.

"You still here?" I said yawning.

"You want me to go?" he asked.

I hugged him to show I didn't. "No, please stay. I just thought after what I did to you at the beach you would hate me."

"A bump on the head. Perhaps it knocked sense into me at last."

I put my fingers to his temple where the bandage oozed blood. "Sorry."

He put his fingers to my temple where the remnants of a scar were still visible. "Sorry, too."

"Why did you come to my room?"

"I knew you were hurting," he said. "Like I hurt."

I made a note to ask him later what he meant for right now I felt his erect cock press into my thigh reminding me that I had not yet had my Greek loving. I slid my hand across his tight muscles giving him an opportunity to stop me at any time before I reached his prick, already wet with pre-cum. I didn't care whether this was a financial transaction, a sympathy fuck or sheer loneliness, I was hungry for love and affection and I was prepared to stoop to any level to get it, even to fucking my enemy. It amused me to realize that I'd already slept with him.

It was difficult to think of someone as your enemy when he has his tongue flicking in your mouth, polishing your teeth and gums with his spit. For someone who had once attacked me, calling me a faggot, Nikos certainly knew how to kiss. He didn't just kiss with his tongue and his lips; he backed it up with his whole being. I had never been kissed like that before. He must be very popular with lonely tourists.

Like me.

I instructed my mind to just lie back and enjoy it. Under normal circumstances, I may have been content just to luxuriate in his kisses all night but the circumstances weren't normal. However, it didn't mean I had to rush. I had no banshee who would call for my obedience from the square. I hoped Nikos wouldn't either and the languid pace of his lovemaking led me to believe he was mine for as long as I wished to keep him. For the night at any rate.

I moved down his body, kissing his neck, lingering over his ink to kiss it, fingering his nipples as I licked across his abs to his cock. It was not as thick as Loukas's but it still made for an ample mouthful and it didn't taste of being with someone else before me. I nuzzled his balls, washing them with my tongue before heading back to his glorious cock jutting up his stomach. I lay on his thigh lazily licking the shaft as he ran his fingers through my hair. Most men at this stage would be pushing my head toward their prick so I could drain their balls, but not Nikos. He seemed content to allow me to do everything in my own time.

When I did finally put my lips around the sensitive head of his cock, he shuddered as if he were the most grateful of men. It was easy to drift from my sucking his cock to his sucking mine, to Nikos pushing my legs over his shoulders as he entered my already lubricated ass. I watched the emotions flicker across his face as he thrust gently into my body and I attempted to make it as memorable as I could. Reaching up to stroke his face, he tenderly took my hand to kiss it.

We were both awash with perspiration when he finally battered my ass into submission, shooting his spunk deep inside me. I realized I'd come to Greece for the wrong man when, after we'd both caught our breath, he offered me his ass. It was so unexpected I almost turned him down but I knew the opportunity would never arise again. He was inexperienced, he told me as much, so I was gentle, more than I really wanted to be, and I made sure I didn't prolong his discomfort for longer than necessary.

If I expected him to flee my room when we'd finished, I was proven wrong. He sat up in the bed, leaning against the chunky wooden bedhead clasping me to his chest. He seemed eager to unburden himself so I remained quiet listening to the beat of his heart.

"I never meant to hurt you, Tommy," he said quietly. "I aimed the stone at Loukas, but you moved just as I threw it."

I was beginning to understand. "You love him."

There was a catch in his throat as he replied. "Yes. All my life. But he is selfish and will only go with men for money. When I spied on him that day when you saw him too, I was so angry with frustration that he would reject me but give his ass up to some old man, I lost control. But you got in the way. I'm sorry."

It was time to let it go. "I understand, Nikos. I forgive you."

"I never forgave myself. I am sorry for six years that I can never explain to you. Loukas forgot you the moment you and your family left the island. He has never thought of you again until I reminded him today."

"He didn't want to come to my room, did he?"

"Not at all. In the end I persuaded him but I knew it would turn out bad, that's why I came to see you."

"He couldn't even remember my name. He kept calling me Bobby."

I laughed at the memory of it.

"Loukas is the reason I didn't leave the island after my mother died. I have stayed around for almost a year in the hope…" He sighed. It was the kind of sigh I'd breathed when I recognized my own stupidity.

I didn't want him to beat himself up over it. "What will you do now?"

"There is nothing for me here. Your visit opened my eyes to what I refused to see before. If I stay it will only mean more pain. He will never love me like I love him."

I tried to leaven the situation with humor. "Anyway, he's getting fat."

"He is," Nikos agreed.

"Your body is a million times better." I rubbed his six-pack in appreciation.

"You like my body?"

"I love your body."

I heard his heart thump hard and fast before he asked his next question. "You love Nikos?"

I was going to answer flippantly but it caught in my throat. I thought about it. "Not yet, but I think I could. Given time."

"I think I am already falling for Tommy."

Shit.

Wait a minute.

"I don't have a lot of money like Loukas's woman friend."

His anger flared for a moment. "I am not like Loukas, I have never gone with men for money. I have enough."

If I didn't ask now, it would lie unspoken between us. "What about women?"

"My body was not made to love women, only men. Men like you, Tommy."

I'd come to Greece with a crazy fantasy, to find love with a tall, dark man from my past. I'd found it not where I expected but in the most unusual of circumstances.

"Will you come with me, Nikos?"

I heard his heart flutter in his chest and he pulled my lips to meet his.

I had all the answer I needed.

Hard On His Heels

"Hello, darlin'. Give us a kiss," some asshole called out of a car as it whizzed by. The occupants of the vehicle weren't even drunk so there was no excuse for their behavior. Plus it was broad daylight. High noon to be exact. Nowhere to hide.

I was walking down the main street of the small country town of Jameson in the verdant Southern Highlands, leading a motley crew of a dozen bears – the human variety not the furry kind, although these guys had plenty of fuzz to go around. They were traipsing behind me as I tottered on high heels that I still was not used to although I'd been wearing them all morning. I held a small rainbow flag on the end of a stick in case any of my group got lost. As if.

There was no way they were going to separate from the main tribe in a town of rednecks, although it had been gentrified over the past ten years and now had a smart café that served vegetarian food and sold organic produce. It was where we'd had lunch, again as a group, making enough noise to attract curious locals and embarrass the hell out of Con, the co-proprietor and boyfriend of Rodney who'd first set up the store. A lot of boisterousness had to do with the fact Con was the spitting image of a Tom of Finland model minus all the leather but with the outline of a cock that made the group's mouths water more than the delicious meals.

Rodney was used to his boyfriend being prodded, poked and panted over and merely smiled indulgently as Con took the group's orders, many of them requesting special meals that weren't listed on the menu but which usually included his cock, balls or bubble butt. It was borderline sexual harassment and I needed to keep a lid on it.

If the town of Jameson had accepted a gay couple in their midst it was because Con was a local lad and popular with it. His dad was a farmer and conservative MP for the area – a conservative MP that actually believed in same-sex equality since his son had come out at the age of seventeen. Rod and Con had met on one of the tours that I was running as part of the Mardi Gras five years earlier. We'd been parading down the main street of the town, much as we were today, when Rodney had spied Con struggling to load a sack of feed onto the back of his lorry. In being a Good Samaritan, Rodney had hooked the area's most eligible bachelor.

A frequent weekend commute had consolidated their friendship over the following few months until they decided to commit to the extent Con told his gobsmacked parents of his gender preference and Rodney put his inner city terrace on the market, moving to the country after settlement had been reached. They'd purchased the small café which became popular with tourists and locals alike. The two men were absorbed into the community so that by the time I started bringing tours, and ready money, into the town on a fortnightly basis in the form of gay and lesbian tour groups we were grudgingly welcomed by most, if not all.

We still ran the gamut of good-natured heckling through homophobic rants from the occasional drunk as we passed the ocker pub. It wasn't unknown for one or more of our group to spend a penny in the toilet in the arcade next door to the café where we ate to discover his oral, anal, or even penile expertise in demand from frustrated, closeted or married locals. Sometimes I wondered if I'd make more money in the area lying flat on my back.

Con and Rodney and their Rainbow Café were not the only reason to stop in the town. Yes, it split the day up nicely. In the morning we'd visited Stanwell Tops – many a tourist thought it amusing to ask where the Stanwell Bottoms were – to watch hang gliders launch themselves off the cliffs over the yellow sandy beaches looking south to Wollongong. Occasionally one of our group thought he was Glinda the Good Fairy and asked to try a flight strapped beneath the hulking body of one of the experts just before they took a running jump. On those occasions, the tally of shrieks of delight ran equal to the shrieks of terror.

The one and only time I managed to pluck up the courage, my mentor managed to rub his crotch into my ass crack before we took off, to show just how friendly he wanted to be. Who am I to turn down friendship when it's offered, even if it's of less than five minutes' duration?

After that the tour heads to Fairy Meadow for a quick walk along the beach which has an uninterrupted view of Wollongong and the belching stacks of Port Kembla. It's also an opportunity for overseas visitors to have their smirking photos taken under the town sign. On to Kiama and the (in)famous Blow Hole. Even the guys with the biggest asses are no match for this fissure in the rock and would drown if that much foam ever hit them full force in the face, although one of the group, Heinz, a solo traveler from Vienna who had already propositioned every man on the tour, boasted he'd taken more sperm at his last party. He was one to watch, and not in a nice way.

That takes us to Jameson where I have been right royally heckled by a carload of hoons, two of which I'm sure I sucked off in the pub dunny many years back during one of the first tours we ran to the area and during which I attempted to play it straight. Yeah, that's like the Pope attempting to pretend he's not wearing a frock. Still, even though the ribbing from the car was good-natured enough, the members of the bear group bunched up for protection.

What were we doing walking down the main street with such a blatant disregard for country life niceties? We were headed for the other reason people stopped in this oasis from the city: Jameson was home to The Big Pea. Pea with an 'a', like Liza with a 'z'. Jameson was the frozen pea capital of the country and to celebrate this momentous achievement, the town council had inaugurated the unveiling of a park dedicated to the economic savior of the area. In Jameson's main park stood the largest concrete green blob in the entire history of the world. It was three-storey's high, there being talk of building a museum inside the structure as well as a staircase to a lookout at the top so people could take photographs of the town and the valleys beyond.

Whether in tribute to the town's indifference or their just plain embarrassment, no funds were ever allocated for the giant pea's upkeep or renovation so it just sat neglected in the center of the park, riddled with concrete cancer, the constant rain leaching the insides through cracks in the shell so that it had lost its round shape and now more resembled a pustule on the verge of bursting than a pea. The color, too, had more in common with pond slime than a giant frozen pea. The ultimate humiliation was the graffiti tags that defaced its lower surface.

I always allowed time for a photo opportunity. Tourists loved having their picture taken lounging over the sign declaring 'Greetings from Jameson – Home of The Big Pea.' Naturally enough, the sign had been regularly tampered with until the council no longer cared enough that their fair town was now The Home of The Big Pee.

Ironic, because the park was the perfect late-night spot for a bit of same-gender liaison, the Giant Pea offering ample protection from prying eyes of traffic on the main road. In fact, on the back side of the 'sculpture' was an area smoothed by some enterprising troll upon which men had solicited for dates, freely admitting their cock size and their preference for sexual positioning. There was also the odd cell phone number. I'd tried them once, but it was an exercise in futility as they were either the local police station after-hours number or the local taxi company.

As the party lined up for their group shot, another carload of rednecks screamed comic abuse at my get-up. It had caused problems all morning, including two men who canceled their booking on seeing me with clipboard and name tag waiting beside the tour bus. "We expected this tour to be professional," the pissier of the two complained before grabbing his partner's hand, dragging him away, shouting over his shoulder, "I hope you're satisfied, you've ruined our day. We'll expect a full refund." As he rounded the nearest corner, he screamed, "And an apology."

The refund we could do, the apology wasn't likely until the day it snowed in Hell.

In case you're wondering, I don't normally dress in drag for my tour duties, be they gay, straight or anything else. It was my own fault, I'd lost a bet earlier in the week on a tour of the wine district. With Dave, who drove the bus. I was so sure of my facts that I bet him I was correct. Bugger! I wasn't. If we'd just bet sex or something similar, the penalty of which could have been paid in private then all would have been well. No, I didn't bet my ass, I bet my utter humiliation. Only because Dave had been giving me the shits that day, adding a few anecdotes about local gay history that I didn't know about.

I forgot, to my peril, that Dave had been born and raised in the area, known for its wine varieties which took out many an international prize. Our sticking point was the first all-lesbian vineyard in the country. It was our second port of call that day for a tasting on our Wine & Cheese Tour. I'd just given a brief run-down on the two women who had created the vineyard and named the shiraz merlot cabinet combination for which they were justly famous. I was in the midst of pontificating about their string of first prizes when I said, "The highlight of the awards was their first place at the 2009 Frankfurt Red Wine Expo."

I was about to go on when there was a snort of derision from Dave and a loud correction, "You mean 2007."

He'd been getting under my skin all day, so I retorted, probably a little fiercer than I intended, "No, I mean 2009."

"Then you're wrong, mate. They didn't enter in 2009 what with the drought and the bushfires."

"That was 2008," I snapped.

He kept his cool which just made me worse. Suddenly, the two of us had everyone's attention in the bus. Then some idiot in the group called, "Why don't you bet on it?"

"I'm game," I said before my mind engaged with my mouth.

Dave whispered, "This is getting silly. We should back off a bit otherwise it could get ugly."

I didn't lower my voice at the suggestion, in fact, I raised it. "Scared you were wrong? Too late to back out now." I turned to the people in the bus. "What should the forfeit be?"

Some dick called out, "Everyone on the bus gets to fuck the loser."

"I don't think Dave's sphincter has seen that much action since World War I," I said, deflecting attention away from the fact my sphincter would never cope with the fifteen tourists on that bus trip plus Dave. Dave was a big enough impost on his own. Not that I didn't have faith in my memory.

"How about the loser has to wear drag on the next tour, regardless of where it's going?" someone else called.

That I could do. Even Dave seemed to breathe easier that his ass wasn't about to receive a real pummeling if he lost. Dave and I accepted that penalty with alacrity.

Turns out I was wrong. First time ever. Dave was not what you'd call magnanimous in victory, especially when I got back to the office of All Out Tours, purveyors of fine holidays to the GLBTIQ gentry, to discover my next group was to Tree-Tops Walkway Rain Forest Resort. The owners were a homophobic bunch of twats who'd threatened to ban our groups as 'disgusting' and a 'danger to families' – their words – but the resort was spectacular and guests could stay overnight. We always took advantage of that option because otherwise it was a mad dash back to the city late at night. It also enabled us to visit some pretty impressive Aboriginal rock paintings, and sneak up on a platypus or two in the wild the next day.

No amount of begging would get Dave to grant me a bit of slack. He was driving for that tour as well so I knew he'd be rubbing my face in my mistake every opportunity he got. Even a plea to the big boss of the company got me nowhere. In fact, he thought he'd like to tag along just to see the looks on their faces when I fronted up at the resort entrance in a frock. I wasn't so sure they'd even let us in. Just in case, we made alternative arrangements although I had to admit the canopy walkway was the highlight of this particular tour.

After we'd explained to our group the reason for my unusual attire and the fact I no longer had a goatee beard and a fuzzy moustache like my photo on the company website, most of them took it in fun, apart from the aforementioned bail-outs.

I'd gone all out with my drag, attempting to look as genuinely female as I could. I didn't want to stand out. Okay, so my faux fur wrap in the middle of summer could have been better chosen. My skirt could have been a little longer but, hey, I'm proud of my legs. And those platform shoes with the high heels really showed off my ass when I walked. I had long hair so I got a friend to style it so it framed my face well and a female friend at the office showed me how to make the best of my complexion with make-up.

I was pretty a-maz-ing, if I say so myself.

We all piled back on the bus at which point I did my spiel as everyone buckled up and got comfortable for the three-hour drive to the rainforest.

I sighed. "Where's Heinz?"

"He said something about needing the toilet, so he ducked into the arcade near the café," one of the Canadians called.

I looked at my watch. I gave him the benefit of the doubt but when he hadn't returned five minutes later, I began to grind my teeth.

"I'll go," Dave volunteered.

"No, you stay here," I ordered. "If the parking police come along, you'd better move. We've overstayed the two-hour limit."

No way could I drive a bus in my shoes.

I disembarked and tottered off to the arcade, attracting stares and whistles as I made my way past shops and open-air eateries. If I'd had the time, I would have taken up some of the salacious invitations – country boys are so cute. But I didn't have time; and I was rapidly running out of patience. Slamming open the door to the men's room, I could hear the tell-tale sounds of someone gagging. He hadn't even paused for breath when he heard my angry entry, always assuming it was Heinz locked in one of the cubicles with the door locked, the old-fashioned bolt showing 'Engaged.'

There was a middle-aged guy at the urinal playing with his cock, obviously waiting his turn, as he listened to the uncensored sounds of oral sex emanating from nearby. He gave a start when he saw me, recovering quickly to wave his cock in my direction. You have to love straight men, they don't really care who they stick their dick in, as long as they can dump a load.

I banged on the closed door of the first cubicle but shouted loudly enough to be heard by just about everyone in town. "The bus is leaving in five minutes, Heinz, with or without you. Four minutes fifty-nine seconds." I marched out of the men's room after giving the gent at the urinal a feel. I'm only human and his cock was a beauty. I'd even toyed with the idea of dropping to my knees to relieve him with my lips and tongue but it was far too dangerous doing it out in the open. Besides, it would dirty my tights.

I stormed back to the bus, keeping a keen eye on my watch. I wasn't sure I had the guts to leave a passenger in a country town with no way of getting back to the city, but I was sorely tempted. As it was, I didn't have to make the decision as Heinz came running, his hair spattered with strings of cum, his jeans tenting from his excitement, and a grin a mile wide pasted on his lips, with five seconds to spare.

It didn't hurt to make him believe we would have left without him. "Just made it," I said.

"I would have been here in plenty of time but you left that poor guy at the urinal with a real problem. I had to help him out." He smacked his lips to show what he meant. Damn, I wanted that guy for myself.

As we passed through the countryside on the way to the rain forest, most of the guys took an opportunity to sleep off their ample meals; they'd mainly sampled kangaroo meat, so they would have something to talk about when they got back home. The bus was quiet and I took the opportunity to catch up on some paperwork as well as ringing the office to report on our progress. I chatted with Dave as he drove through the afternoon, keeping our voices low so as not to disturb the group.

I got up to ensure the passengers were wearing their seat belts, something that was dictated by law and which could see the company served with severe penalties if we were caught napping in this regard.

There seemed to be some unusual activity about midway down the bus, those people in surrounding seats taking a great interest in what was occurring on one of the double seats. As I approached no one appeared embarrassed or did anything out of the ordinary so I guessed people were talking quietly amongst themselves.

Not so. As I got closer, I noticed Heinz's head was bobbing up and down as he faced the front of the bus. It wasn't the seat he'd been sitting in previously although that was no matter as people shifted constantly, making new friends. However, that was the two seats in which a newly married gay couple from New York had been holding hands earlier. One of them was looking out the window, distress contorting his face. I discovered why when I got closer: Heinz was impaled on the New Yorker's husband, riding his cock like a whirlwind. Those passengers around them were engrossed in the free live porn show.

Sure, I could have enforced the seatbelt rule but what would that have achieved? I watched for a few moments as the New Yorker's rather thick cock sloshed into Heinz's welcoming butthole. I had to give it to the Austrian, his cock was a work of art. If I hadn't found him so repugnant I probably would have made a play for him myself. As it was I merely tapped the miserable guy watching his lover's infidelity reflected in the bus window and pointed to Heinz's cock. "That's a mighty fine cock going to waste there." I indicated Heinz's leaking dick. "What's good for the goose…" I left it at that.

I'm not sure whether the cuckold had insufficient imagination or was so distraught he hadn't thought of it, but once I'd pointed out the availability of a nice piece of meat, he swallowed it in one mouthful.

"Seat belts back on when you've finished, gents," I said quietly as I continued down the aisle.

I went back to my position at the front of the bus, noting that Heinz shared his ass with another three passengers before clicking on his seat belt. I could see there'd be a lot of room swapping at the resort that evening.

The resort! My stomach got fluttery. I wasn't looking forward to it. It wasn't the physical resort itself that was the concern, it was our reception. The property itself was several dozen hectares of lush rain forest with pleasant walking trails, the native flora signposted, the opportunity to see native animals such as wombats, lyrebirds, koalas, possums, snakes, cockatoos, and owls minimal but at least people were walking through their natural habitat. Closer to the overnight cabins were picnic areas, children's playgrounds, barbecue areas, a spa, a sauna, and a swimming pool. You could opt for a massage from one of the professionals or you could take horse riding lessons through the native forest.

The highlight, of course, was the metal walkway that jutted from the edge of the escarpment about twenty-five meters above the forest floor through the gum trees and other native plants until it was at canopy height among the top leaves of the tress at seventy-five meters above the ground. There were spectacular views to the coast from the highest point.

The walkway was safe as trees although it swayed as people walked along the various metal pathways. Occasionally, young kids, their face a rictus grin of fear as they were dragged reluctantly toward an appreciation of nature reminded me of the first time I set foot on the structure. I wondered if the metal poles anchored into the forest floor were enough to support a group's combined weight even though I was assured the structure could withstand everything nature could throw at it, including a group of gay men or gale-force winds.

As we approached the entrance to the resort, I took a deep breath, anticipating the worst.

"I can book us in, if you like," Dave volunteered.

It was a kind offer, but I'd have to face the music eventually.

Dave dropped me and the guys at the front entrance while he took the bus to find a spot to park overnight. I'd warned the group not to make a fuss over any homophobic provocation if they wanted to see the rain forest, to be met with a chorus of sniggers as they looked at my outfit. They had a point. Pushing open the door, I was sending a silent prayer to whatever gods looked after the rain forest to help protect us. To my delight, they must have heard me for behind the counter was an Aboriginal ranger I'd never seen before.

He looked me up and down and instead of the sneer I expected, he smiled. "What have we here?" He consulted the ledger on the front counter. "You must be Seth and this is your bear group in town for Mardi Gras. Welcome, gentlemen."

This was a surprise. After the formality of signing the register and generally getting a quick orientation of the resort, I sent the group to their rooms, suggesting they grab a coffee or use the men's room before meeting back at the front entrance in thirty minutes.

I waited for the key to my cabin. "What's happened to…" I named the bastards who I'd had trouble with on previous occasions.

"Haven't you heard?" Sonny the ranger said.

"Heard what? We took this place off our list after we had problems with the owners. We've only just started to come back."

"The resort went bankrupt. The owners antagonized so many people, it went broke. The government bought it dirt cheap and handed it over to us."

"Us who?"

"The local Aboriginal people. Or what's left of us. We've managed to turn it around. Introduced a lot of new attractions. People seem to like what we've done with it."

"So, this…" I drew attention to my outfit.

"Not a problem," he shrugged. "I'd lose the fur though; it's hot as buggery in the forest."

Sonny handed me the key but kept his fingers in the palm of my hand for longer than I thought necessary but not as long as I would have liked. "If you don't mind a word of advice."

Here it comes, I thought.

"Take your group out on the walkway this afternoon. They're predicting rain tomorrow. Not so pleasant then."

I was genuinely surprised. "Thanks, I'll do that." I turned my biggest smile on him, almost tripping over my own feet in my vain effort to impress.

By the time we regrouped half an hour later, Sonny had disappeared but an equally charming young woman handed us all our kits which included a bottle of water, a spotter's guide, information on the various plants, and a map highlighting the towns and coastal cities we'd observe from the walkway.

Rather than meander through the forest to the viewing platform that was the entrance to the metal pathway, we made our way straight there. Time enough tomorrow to linger over the native plants. There were already a number of family groups with children on the walkway which meant it swayed more than usual, resulting in two of our group bailing out, saying they would walk the trail and meet us at the disembarkation point. I didn't blame them; I'd been overcome with vertigo on my first attempt as well. The difference was that I'd had to overcome it as I was the guide.

A number of other visitors attached themselves to our group, whether attracted by my commentary or my outrageous dress sense I wasn't sure, but provided they didn't push their way to the front of the pack I didn't mind letting them tag along.

About ninety minutes later we reached the end of the aerial track and we grouped for a head count. Bloody Heinz was missing. The last he'd been seen was with a group of men about the half-way point on our ramble. I'd a good mind to leave him but, as the sun was setting and it was difficult to find your way back in the dark, I thought I'd better go looking for him.

Dave took the remainder of the group back for dinner while I stormed off in my high heels. I was fuming, determined to give Heinz a real blast. As a result I wasn't looking where I was going when two teenage boys, more interested in the sway of the walkway than the nature surrounding it, bumped into me as they ran past so that I slipped, catching the heel of my shoe in the grate, twisting my ankle painfully.

Bloody high heels on a metal grate. What was I thinking?

I hauled myself up as best I could but screamed when I put pressure on my foot. My ankle was already beginning to swell alarmingly. I knew panic was the enemy, so I extracted my cell phone and went to dial Dave to come and get me. They had golf carts to pick up people like me. No luck. There was no signal. Oh, great!

I was not concerned as there'd be another sightseer along at any moment and they could go for help. You remember the rain that Sonny the ranger had warned about for the next day? Well, it arrived an evening early. The dark clouds had blown in from the coast while we'd been too busy gawking at the views. The waning sun disappeared and the temperature dropped. Now I wished I'd brought my faux fur after all. I wrapped my hands around my upper body in an attempt to stay warm.

Spots of rain fell, plinking against the metal. It was no good remaining here at the mercy of the elements. I attempted to stand again, hobbling a few steps before I fell head first onto the walkway. The unladylike expletive that exploded from my mouth echoed across the valley. Perhaps if I tried crawling. The metal grate dug into my knees and my hands until they began to bleed. I was doomed. I was going to die in wilting drag on the canopy walkway in a national park. What a way to go. I was going to come back and haunt Dave for the ridiculous bet we'd both made. If I survived, I was gonna cut Heinz up into fifty-seven different varieties and stick each piece in a can.

I tried calling but anyone with any sense had already fled for shelter; the rain was now pelting down. I must have looked a real wreck. I knew I wasn't really going to die up here; someone would miss me and send out the rangers to find me. It was just a matter of waiting. Provided I didn't suffer from hypothermia, I'd be okay. I snuggled my body as best I could into a sort of fetal crouch to make myself a smaller target for the rain. I must have fallen asleep because when I awoke, it was pitch black. I could not see my hand in front of my face. The wind had come up and the metal walkway was creaking as it was buffeted this way and that.

Off in the distance I thought I heard my name called. I yelled as loudly as I could but with the swooshing of the tree branches and the thud of the rain I doubt anyone could hear me. Then, if I listened carefully, I thought I could hear the faint clank of someone walking on the metal bridge.

"Over here," I called, cupping my hands around my mouth.

I heard a call in response. I shouted again but the wind was making it hard to pinpoint my location. Then I saw the beam of a flashlight in the distance. I grabbed my phone and began to knock it against the metal railing above my head hoping the vibration, if not the sound, would be apparent to my rescuer. The light was moving closer. I'm afraid I got a little hysterical, screaming and banging my phone until the light turned in my direction, picking me out huddled against the railing.

"Over here," I heard a voice call.

Then there were hands helping me to my feet, someone swept me into his strong arms when I screamed in agony with my foot. Just before I passed out from cold and pain, I was professional enough to ask whether Heinz had made it back.

"Is that the German?" a familiar voice asked.

"Austrian."

"Whatever." Sonny laughed. "He chatted up every male ranger when he got back to the resort. Made a mistake with Kevin. Came on a bit too strong and Kevin gave him a split lip. He'll probably complain about brutality and homophobia, but Kevin's gay. It's just he has a boyfriend and he's very faithful."

I seem to recall I asked, "What about you? You got a boyfriend?" but I was unconscious before I heard an answer.

It was daylight outside, the rain seemingly blowing itself out overnight, when I woke up in the cabin. I was in bed, Naked. Someone had undressed me and put me under the blankets to keep warm. I shivered, I had a cold coming on, but I was safe. I glanced at my cell phone for the correct time. Shit! I was late. I sat up but my head spun and I had to lie down again or I would have fallen out of the bed. I must have groaned because a voice came from the living room. "You're awake then?"

"If you can call this awake," I replied.

Sonny came in. "How are you feeling?"

"Can you help me up? I have a group to take around."

"Don't sweat it, mate. They're up and out already. Dave has taken over. Your best bet is to take it easy today. That foot of yours is so swollen there's no way you'll be walking on that for a week or more."

I looked around, everything was unfamiliar. "Where am I?"

"You're in my cabin," he said.

"When did we get married?" I joked.

"It's more comfortable than your room. I hope you don't mind."

"You undressed me?"

"The doctor helped."

"What doctor?"

"We had to call him in. You were in a bad way out there."

"Did he have his wicked way with me?"

"If you saw the doc, you wouldn't ask that."

"Did…um…you?"

"Nah. That's not to say I wasn't tempted. You're a fine looking specimen. For a city boy. But necrophilia's not my style."

"So, you're gay?"

"One hundred and ten per cent."

I swallowed hard. "Boyfriend?"

"You asking will I be your boyfriend or do I have a boyfriend?"

"Oh, what the hell? Both?"

"No, I don't have a boyfriend at present. But I am looking."

"I'd like to volunteer." I smirked.

"Don't think much of your fashion sense."

I blustered. "That was all a stupid bet…"

"Don't bust a gasket. Dave's explained it all." He laughed and the sound filled the room.

"Come here."

Sonny came over and lay on the bed beside me.

"You believe in love at first sight?" I asked.

"You're still delirious," he replied, placing his hand on my forehead to see if I had a fever.

I pulled him down so that our lips touched. I prized his mouth open in order to slip my tongue inside. I felt his reluctance until I was fully inside his mouth. He sighed, relaxing into my embrace.

I love kissing and Sonny proved as adept at it as he was at saving my ass. I hated it when he released me and got up from the bed.

"Don't go," I begged.

"I'm not going anywhere," he said, stripping off his clothes before climbing under the blankets with me, his hard cock pressing insistently against my leg. I ran my hand down over his chest and through his bushy pubes until I wrapped my hand around it.

"I want you to fuck me," I pleaded.

"I want to, mate. More than anything. But not while your foot is the way it is. How about we settle for this?"

He pulled the blankets up over his head and I felt his tongue inch its way down my torso until he engulfed my aching prick in his hot mouth.

"Shit, that's good. Suck me, Sonny."

I think he said 'No problem' but what with the blankets muffling his voice and my cock filling his mouth, I'm not sure.

He siphoned me off expertly. I felt guilty that I couldn't reciprocate but he sat astride my chest as he jerked himself all over my face, leaning forward to lick me clean before we swapped the juice between us.

"That's just the beginning," he promised.

"Pity I have to go back to the city this afternoon," I said miserably.

"Nah, mate," Sonny smiled. "The doctor insisted you can't be moved. Not for a week at least. Dave is taking the group back and he'll pick you up next time he brings more people through. Your company wants you to make a full recovery."

"Can I can stay with you?"

"That goes without saying, mate," Sonny said. "I insist."

Salted Mixed Sluts

Luke Hoenig's the name and I'm hot. Not as in the handsome-with-a-killer-body way – although I'm that, too – but as in the excess of warmth. I ducked into the faux beach-hut design café to take advantage of the air conditioning and their wicked triple espresso, made just the way I liked it: enough of a caffeine hit to heart start an elephant. I'm no elephant: I am a trim, tanned and terrific surfer boy who is spending his gap year searching for the world's biggest and best waves.

I'd heard through the surfer grape vine about the Demon Curl of Shark Bay. The Demon Curl was legendary and I'd sought it all my surfing life, never expecting to find it in such an unprepossessing spot; a picturesque and as yet unspoiled hamlet on the north coast. As I was headed in that general direction it was no hardship to make a slight detour to see the conditions for myself.

I'd been in the town for three days and, apart from the demon coffee, I'd been heartily disappointed. The surf in the tiny enclave had not lived up to the whispered hype. Truth is, I was tired of the constant travel. I'd been searching for the perfect wave for six months so far, with little success. I'd palled up with various groups on my journey but those friendships were fleeting and washed off much like sand washed off my body in the surf. I'd had some fun but it was a lonely existence.

For all the connotations of its name no one had ever been taken by one of the sea predators at Shark Bay and I had hoped it would prove amenable in both surf and salvation. I'd been disappointed in both. The surf was as flat as the asphalt main street that housed the Beach Hut café and the meager supply of bait and tackle shops, the boat hire, the pub and the general store-cum-post office.

Normally, I had no problem getting my knob polished on a regular basis but the local chicks proved stand-offish even though I turned on my killer charm, so I was in serious danger of blue balls. Other surfers in the town had split into cliques but none of them seemed keen on admitting me to their ranks. One group in particular – all locals I discovered subsequently – were particularly belligerent, as if they had a proprietorial interest in the waves in the area. They always disappeared with their boards strapped to the roofs of their off-road vehicles after a noisy breakfast in the café.

At the end of a dispiriting first day on the beach where I, along with other disappointed surfers, had watched an ocean as flat as a geek's chest, I was pissed off to overhear the locals boasting of the waves they'd discovered a little way along the coast. Obviously they were not the caring and sharing type. I could live with that.

The next day I made sure I was at the café at sparrow's fart, ready to follow at a respectable distance when the locals headed off with their superior knowledge of the area. I kept a safe distance behind so they couldn't see me although I lost them on a number of occasions and had to double back. If they'd been tour guides they could not have done a better job of showing me the highlights of the coastal area but I was too obsessed with the perfect wave and keeping track of my quarry to really notice the scenery.

It turned out to be a wasted day. They drove around for hours, visiting pub after pub while I sat in my sweltering car, 'air conditioning' courtesy of an open window, eating greasy burgers and drinking lukewarm soda while they yahooed in cold comfort with an icy beer. I was so wrapped up in discovering their secret surfing beach it never occurred to me that they were on to my shadowing activities. At least, not until the end of the day when they turned around and headed back to Shark Bay. Once I realized what was going on I headed for the four-lane expressway in disgust while they took the more scenic but meandering coastal road.

I was angry with them, I was angry with myself. I was also frustrated, bored and lonely. I had just about made up my mind to head back home to get myself a job so I had a little cash for uni the next year. Better that than the nagging dejection souring in my stomach. I slammed into the café, determined to leave the next morning, almost taking the wire door used to keep out the flies off its hinges.

A few customers smirked when they looked up to discover it was 'just me' before going back to whatever activity they were engaged in. My face reddened as I realized what a twat I'd made of myself. I was a laughing stock. I ordered at the counter and then headed to one of the booths in the darkest corner of the café for a little privacy. It was the weekend tomorrow and there would be an influx of city surfers looking for sun, surf and sex. Let the locals find themselves another target. I was out of there.

Leaving my jacket in the booth to show it was occupied I headed for the men's room to relieve my bladder of all that soda I'd guzzled in a fruitless effort to keep cool while on watch. It was an orgasm-strength relief to empty my piss tank. Yes, I washed my hands before heading back to my calamari.

As I slid into the booth, I heard the sound of voices over the partition in the booth next to mine. It was the guys I'd been following all day. They made no secret that they were laughing at my expense although they had no way of knowing I was seated behind them overhearing every embarrassing word of how they'd outfoxed me.

"Oh, man, what a fuckin' boring day," one of them said. "I hope we're not going to repeat it tomorrow."

"Nah, he'll head up north tomorrow is my bet, too chicken to show his face."

"Just in case, I reckon we should head off earlier. Before he comes into the Beach Hut for his..." the speaker put on a voice that made me out to be a prat, "triple espresso. 'It's the best I've had outside the city.' Patronizing bastard."

"I don't know why we can't share what info we've got with him," one voice said. "It's not like we have to talk to him if we don't want to. Lightning Cove is big enough for all of us."

The others tried to shut him up in case anyone overheard the name of their secret beach.

Too late, I thought.

"Weather report for tomorrow is for wicked surf."

"Maybe we'll be lucky and see the Devil's Curl."

"That would be awesome."

Their conversation dwindled into commonplace gossip and I lost interest although I was keen to see which of them had been generous of spirit enough to suggest sharing the beach with me. It was impossible without giving away my proximity. I waited for them to leave before I paid my bill, deciding to head for the pub before turning in for the night.

I'd put my escape plans on hold to check out this mysterious beach with waves so high they could send you to hell and back. I could have been a bastard and revealed the secret beach name to the weekend surfers who were already pouring into the town from the city, having escaped their weekday drudgery early enough to beat the traffic, but I didn't.

The pub was crowded already but after getting myself a cold beer I managed to find a stool in a corner so I could survey the bar. I found my quarry straight away because they were arrogant enough, being locals, that they thought their opinions were worth more than those of visitors and, therefore, made them known at decibels high enough to be heard throughout the venue. For once, I was pleased by their arrogance because it gave me a chance to put voice to face.

When I had first arrived in the town, I took them to be your typical surfer dudes and had paid little attention to them as individuals. Now that I'd suffered their contempt, I examined them more closely. They were young, brash and confident, comfortable in their youth and popularity. Not bad looking dudes, but nothing earth shattering either. They were tanned, their hair bleached by sun and saltwater, their bodies slim and muscular, not much excess fat on any of them.

Eventually, he spoke. He wasn't one for extraneous conversation or opinions so I'd waited ten minutes or so before I heard his voice enough that I could match it to the more kindly conversation in the café. Maybe it was my bias because of his less belligerent attitude to sharing his beach but to my mind he was easily the blondest and best looking of the gang. He wore baggy board shorts and a colored singlet, though what color it had been before it had bleached with perspiration, sand and surf, I wasn't sure. He had eyes so piercing blue I could see them across the bar. His arms, covered in a fine blond fur, were those of someone used to manual labor because his biceps stood out. This guy would be a favorite with the chicks. Lucky bastard.

I was hoping to pick up his name and, as a result, I guess I was staring a little too fixedly at him when he looked up from his beer and saw me. I expected a sneer of contempt, a whisper to his mates, a finger, anything but the wry smile that played about his lips before his focus was pulled back to his companions. None of them had noticed our brief exchange.

WTF was that smile? Shit-eating superiority? I couldn't work it out. He'd seemed so onside in the overheard conversation, but now that lip movement… was it meant to signify something? I couldn't interpret the signal if, indeed, it was a signal at all. I didn't have the same manual he was working from.

Hell, what did it matter? I waited until one of his mates addressed him as 'Tick' before I quickly finished my beer and headed back to the Bed & Breakfast where I'd paid for the room until the following Tuesday in expectation of cunt and companionship if not waves and wanking. I found old Mrs. Baker, the proprietress and told her I'd overheard a few of the locals mentioning the great waves at Lightning Cove.

"Oh, you don't want to go there, love," she said good-naturedly.

"But I overheard some of the local boys raving about it," I argued.

"Well, you don't want to believe everything you overhear."

"What's wrong with the beach?" I insisted.

"It's…" She hesitated to gather her words. "Look, love, it's dangerous to the likes of you."

The likes of me? Did she mean the locals would attack someone from out of town in order to keep their secret safe? Sure I'd heard tales about human sacrifices in other parts of the world, but at the beach? It was too ludicrous to contemplate.

"Dangerous? How?" I asked.

"I've already said too much," she whispered as one of her permanent guests came into the lounge area.

I wasn't about to let her put me off. "Where is this mysterious beach?" I asked.

She sighed. "Don't say I didn't warn you, love." She looked me up and down. "Very well. You're a big lad. You look like you can take care of yourself. I'll tell you, but mind you don't reveal the source of your information." She tapped the side of her nose.

She whispered the whereabouts of the beach and the route by which I could get there in the morning. It sounded easy enough although she reiterated that I needed to take care because it was dangerous to people like me.

I admit she spooked me with all her talk of danger and the conspiratorial manner in which the local populace guarded Lightning Cove's secret. That's what probably affected my dreams that night: that or the anticipation of meeting the Devil's Curl. My dreams, like my sleep, were fragmented. I made little sense of the snippets I remembered. However, one image kept reoccurring no matter how surreal the dreams: that of a pair of the deepest blue eyes and a curled up mouth that scored its Cheshire Cat-like replica into my memory.

Of course, I recognized it as Tick's enigmatic smile across the bar earlier in the evening. I was only slightly non-plussed that my cock was hard as steel in the morning, after all I'd been dreaming of a bloke for God's sake, but I always woke up with a piss hard-on. Even when I didn't need to piss. If I'd had more time to think it all through, I may have been more concerned but I had tracks to make, waves to ride, locals to thumb my nose at. Maybe, I'd see Tick…

Where the fuck had that thought come from?

The Beach Hut opened early on weekends to get the surfer trade before it headed off to various locations. It did great business in take-away because many of the secluded coves and sandy beaches had nothing in the way of amenities. I grabbed one of their ready-made boxed lunches because I had no idea what time I'd be back, a couple of bottles of water and my usual triple espresso to go.

I bobbed about impatiently, hoping I was way ahead of my tormentors. I wanted to stake my claim before they arrived. Yeah, I know, pathetic but it gave my being there more legitimacy than if I gate crashed 'their' beach when they were already on site. Besides, it might look as if I'd followed them.

I checked with the Sat Nav in the car but it had none of the local roads, little more than tracks in the sand, listed. I was careful to follow the instructions Mrs. Baker had revealed and was pleasantly surprised she was better than any electronic navigation system. She'd given me the inside goss on local conditions so I made good time even in the sections on which she'd warned of problems. I was feeling very pleased with myself when I got to the area where she told me I would have to park the car to make my way on foot. There were already half a dozen cars parked among the tea trees and I maneuvered mine beneath another in order to disguise it as best I could from the guys in the café when they turned up and also to protect the car as much as possible from what would be the stinking hot midday sun.

I didn't notice any vehicles belonging to the local surfers although I was surprised by the number that were already there. The area looked as if some people had spent the night sleeping on the ground or else in their cars. There were no boards strapped to the roofs, so I had to assume everyone was on the beach.

It was from this point on, so Mrs. Baker stressed, that things got dangerous. I took my time expecting the worst, but the trail down the side of the steep incline was no worse than many I'd traversed to get to out-of-the-way beaches. Sure, it was an unrailed pathway, worn into the sandy soil by countless people like myself, which meandered down the side of the cliff with only flattened scrub to cling on to for support. It was especially difficult while carrying a board. The vertiginous drop should I lose my footing gave me brief pause as I set off but Mrs. Baker had mentioned nothing about casualties so I took comfort from that.

Occasionally, I caught a glimpse of a naked male amongst the bushes and trees off to the sides but they had to have been men taking a piss or a dump in private. I marveled at their stamina in choosing such a precipitous open-air lavatory but I guessed there was little privacy on the beach itself.

Every now and then, someone had obligingly cut crude steps into the rock which made the descent easier although there's no way Health & Safety would ever approve this trail for general tourists. I didn't run into anyone on the path itself apart from the glimpses off to the side so I was unprepared for the numbers when I finally reached the beach itself. There was upwards of a dozen men already lounging on towels soaking up the warm morning sun before it became too hot and toasted their skin. There were men, too, jumping about in the waves. The flat-as-a-pancake waves. Not the giant surf monsters I was expecting. I told myself it was early yet.

What stood out on the sand was not so much that some of the surfers had obviously spent the night on the beach, witnessed by the number of charcoal pits, or that I was the only person with a board. No, the biggest surprise was that every other man, and they were all men, was stone bollock naked.

I know blond hair and saltwater are supposed to signify a certain lack of intelligence but even I could see this was a gay beach, especially after I watched a number of men holding hands, or kissing in a more than matey fashion, but especially after three guys got a little frisky and…well, let's just say, it involved a number of penises, a mouth and an ass.

I've got nothing against gay guys, but you don't run into them all that often in the surfing fraternity in what is a pretty homophobic sport. That's not to say there aren't any but they keep very much to themselves or mix with their own kind in groups. Others stay in the closet with the door wedged tightly shut. I had suspected early on that the local surfing mafia may have mistaken me for gay.

I'd been hit on more than a few times by gay surfers but there'd always been enough stray pussy to keep me happy. I didn't have any great argument against sticking my dick in some dude's mouth or even in his shit hole, I'd done both those things with enough chicks. I just didn't fancy the idea of a dick up my own hole, even after one of my longer-term girlfriends had increased the power of my orgasms by sticking her finger in my butt when I was about to blow. She said the gush of spunk almost blew her head off when I came in her mouth with her finger poking my prostate.

It did occur to me that the bastards in the café had set me up, knowing I was in the booth behind them. Overhearing their private conversation about spectacular waves at Lightning Cove could pretty much guarantee I'd head there today. I still held out the forlorn hope that maybe it was for real, even as I sat on my towel, more dejected that I had been in years. People glared at me as they strolled past. I didn't seem to fit in anywhere.

Then I remembered: not only was it a gay beach but it seemed to be a nude beach and I was the only person wearing clothes. I didn't want to encourage familiarity because cocks weren't my strong suit. Sure, mine was okay – I'd never had any complaints – but that didn't mean I wanted it flapping in the breeze. Shit, what did I have to lose?

I'd give these gay guys a show. I stood to slowly peel my singlet up and over my head, running my hands across my six-pack and tweaking my nipples until they were hard. I was snickering at my audacity while the cotton vest covered my face when I heard a number of wolf whistles and a few calls of 'Take it all off.' Unfortunately, my cock rather liked the idea and suddenly started to fill with blood, tenting obviously in my board shorts.

A small group had gathered rather closer than I was comfortable with, but it was too late to hunt them away. They were all in various stages of erection so my stiff cock was not about to shock them. There was something liberating about showing off. Chicks didn't behave like this; some guys openly groping themselves or their mates while I did my strip act. There was no denying I was horny as fuck. I watched as one muscular guy dropped to his knees and suctioned a rather large cock all the way down his throat without gagging. My prick started to drool at the idea.

I'd never ever thought about a blow job from a guy before although I'd heard tales of surfer dudes too drunk to care allowing a gay guy to siphon the python. Big difference: I wasn't drunk.

"Come on, dude," begged one of the onlookers, "show us what you got."

It was a good feeling to be accepted even if these guys were ogling my superficial qualities. Who was I kidding? That's all the chicks wanted me for, too. After the past few days of being all but ignored and ridiculed by the locals it was fun to be the center of attention of these horny city boys. That's what they were, I was convinced of it. They may covet my cock or my ass, but a strip and tell was about all they were going to get.

But I'd make it a good one. I swiveled my hips like a demented belly dancer to the cheers and applause of the onlookers which merely encouraged more guys to join the crowd. I lowered my board shorts down over my hips revealing the top of my ass crack. That sent a few of them wild and more than a shiver up my spine. The bubble of my butt cheeks and the roaring steel of my solid prick were the only things holding my shorts in place.

Did I dare? Hell, yeah. I peeled the fabric over my smooth butt which had a little blond down trail in my ass crack. I heard a few groans of appreciation and noticed a few guys leisurely stroking their pricks. No one seemed particularly perturbed about a visit by the cops. I guess there was no way they'd want to chance that cliff face with more than a dozen gay guys under arrest.

Turning my back to the crowd, I bent over to tug my shorts free and kick them off. My asshole was probably visible for a moment and I wondered if any of the guys found it attractive enough to fuck. I didn't wonder long as a few of the more vocal members told me what they wanted to do with that snug, tight hole and the most commonly used word was 'plow.'

Totally naked now, with my cock still hidden, I slowly stood to my full height, flexing my arms behind my head for maximum effect and turned to face my admirers, my cock harder than it had ever been before in my life. It slapped against my stomach as I turned, smearing snail trails of cum slime across my belly. I knew I was a success by the gaping mouths and the flames of desire revealed in their eyes. Suddenly, I wondered if I were in danger from being gang fucked by a hoard of randy gay men.

We all needed to cool off. Me included. I don't know what got into me to be so indiscreet. I wasn't gay. I didn't want to have sex with these men although I had no problems with them using me to feed their beat-off fantasy. I saw my chance and took it, racing down the beach, my cock flapping, sticky with ooze, until I plunged into the cool embrace of the ocean. A number of guys tore down the beach after me, splashing and rubbing against me like little kids would do in an attempt to impress. Others tried chatting me up. It was interesting to see dudes were much more direct when propositioning other dudes. I didn't take offence; after all, I'd encouraged it.

When they discovered I was straight, a few sneered 'prick tease' and wandered off while others believed they had what it takes to 'convert' me. Very unlikely. I was disappointed when I found myself totally abandoned although I realized how much I'd missed the water even if it were as placid as a stagnant pond. I swam out a little way, not venturing too far as I didn't know the beach well and didn't want to be carried away in a rip.

I felt something brush my body and wondered momentarily if Shark Beach, a few miles down the coast, was aptly named. Sharks, however, rarely put their hand around a surfer's cock. At least not in any books I'd read.

I allowed him to grope my more than handful as I waited for him to surface. I should not have been surprised when he came up for breath.

"You showed up then?"

I was gazing into the bluest eyes I'd ever seen.

I laughed, a little too heartily because I swallowed a little seawater.

"You bastard," I smiled. "You set me up, didn't you?"

"Guilty," he said sheepishly.

"Why?"

We trod water and swam around each other slowly heading back to the shore.

"I guess I wondered if you were gay."

"Sorry, I'm straight."

He gasped. "Impossible. After that exhibition you put on?"

I blushed crimson. "You saw that?"

"I was sooo hard for your ass," he admitted. "Oh, sorry, is that offensive."

"I'd be lying if I said it was. I guess it's nice to hear someone finds you desirable."

"Oh, come on," he said. "The entire beach finds you desirable. Don't you know how cute you are?"

"Cute? Not sure a straight man likes to hear himself described as 'cute'." I was only mock serious. Coming from Tick I found I rather liked it.

We'd reached the shore and made our way up the beach to where my surf board lay in the sand with my towel. I spread it out to lie down to let the sun dry me off.

"Mind if I join you?" Tick asked. "I promise I'll behave."

"I'd like that," I said.

He raced farther up the beach and soon returned with his own towel spreading it alongside mine.

"It's Tick, isn't it?"

"Yeah, I made sure you heard that much in the bar after I saw you staring at me."

"I wasn't…yes, I was staring. I'd never seen eyes like yours."

"Thanks. I think."

"It was a compliment. So, you guys knew I was in the booth behind you at the Beach Shack?"

"Yeah. The others wanted to get physical in a nasty way but I said it would be better to humiliate you by sending you on a wild goose chase the next day to the gay beach. That got the thumbs up."

"Not exactly gay friendly the circle you mix with?"

"Anything but."

"They don't know about you then?"

"Nah. I have just enough girlfriends to throw them off the scent."

"You aren't worried that I'll reveal all?"

"Nah, you seem like a nice guy for a straight. I guess I'll have to trust you."

"It must be lonely."

"It's okay. I come down here from time to time and meet up with someone and we head off to the bushes or maybe make out in the car."

"Not much of a life."

"I'm moving away next year. Going to uni. My folks wanted me to stay in the town but there's no future here. Not for the likes of me, at any rate."

"Why Tick?"

"You mean the name?"

I nodded.

"Bit stupid really. Once I get something into my head I'm a stubborn bastard and I'm about as hard to shift as a tick. And just as aggravating."

"I like it," I smiled.

"You may not like it so much when I tell you my latest plan."

"Yeah? What is it?"

I was lying with my arm across my eyes to protect them from the sun. When he didn't answer at once, I opened them to see him staring down into my face. It was the vision I'd seen in my dreams.

I couldn't breathe; I thought my heart had stopped. His mouth found mine and his tongue snaked between my lips before I even thought to stop him. By then it was too late. His lips were soft as they rubbed against me, his tongue caressing the inside of my mouth as he gently prodded my own somnambulant tongue to engage with his. I was so surprised by how good it felt I relaxed and allowed him to take charge, fascinated that kissing Tick was even better than the perfunctory oral ministration of most women I'd made out with.

It wasn't only my mouth that was enjoying the experience; my cock decided it wanted to get in on the action.

"Mmm," I murmured when he broke for breath. "Your kisses are magic."

"You didn't mind?"

"Not at all," I admitted. "It's not something I thought I'd like but now that it's done, well…"

"Can I do it again?" he asked eagerly.

"Will it make me gay?" I asked facetiously.

"It might."

"I'll take a chance."

Our kiss was more aggressive, more masculine this time as I kissed back rather than accepting it passively in surprise as I had the first time. He was on top although our bodies scarcely touched but I ran my hands down his body thrilled by the silky feel of his skin and his buttocks. My cock knew it was a man's ass I was squeezing and it didn't care. I only wished my brain felt the same way.

I was sorry when we broke again to breathe and he lay back down on his towel, his one-word response being, "Wow."

We were silent for a while before we were comfortable enough to ask the sorts of questions two guys ask when they smell out the possibility of a new friend. Or maybe the sorts of questions you ask when you're on a first date.

The subject of sex was broached in the most general of terms, both of us admitting we'd had many partners but never found the right girl or, in his case, boy, although we were both looking.

We had so much in common it was inevitable that somewhere during our lengthy conversation I'd admitted, "If only you were a girl," and he'd responded with, "If only you were gay."

Neither of us was sure how long we'd been swapping personal histories when the ominous rumble of thunder rolled in across the now choppy waves. Glancing around we noticed the clouds had turned quite dark and were rapidly threatening to blot out the sun. Many bathers had already left the beach and more were gathering up their clothes and towels in order to flee the approaching electrical storm.

"I guess we better move," Tick said. "The storms here can be fierce."

"Is that why it's called Lightning Cove?" I asked.

He nodded. "During a bad storm the area lights up like a fireworks display. It's a sight to see."

"Will we make the top of the cliff before it hits?"

Tick looked at the clouds, then said seriously. "Unlikely. You don't want to be caught out in the open here. Come on, we need to move it."

By this time there were few hardy souls still milling about on the beach.

Tick called to them that they needed to seek shelter as the storms could be lethal. He pointed a short distance away to an overhang of rock that offered protection. Men were already huddled there to wait out the storm.

I grabbed my board while Tick took my towel and my clothes as well as our packed lunches before we made a dash for it as a slash of light illuminated the beach to be followed by a growl of thunderous disapproval. The rain bucketed down just before we reached shelter and by the time we joined the half dozen or so other men under the rock's protective embrace we were soaked. It didn't matter we were naked as I hadn't felt so alive in ages. The air was positively electric with…what was it? Passion? Possibilities? Whatever it was, my body tingled.

Another three men ran in from the storm as the rain came down so thickly that it was impossible to see the waves. We moved farther toward the back of the cave to avoid the damp and the cold. The temperature had dropped precipitously and some of us wrapped our arms about ourselves to keep warm, everyone seemingly reluctant to put their clothes back on. We all lay our towels together to form a strangely patterned picnic blanket. Without anyone suggesting it, those of us who had brought food placed it in the center so we could all share. I enjoyed sitting with Tick, comfortable enough in his presence to lean against his body, not at all embarrassed when my cock got hard. Others paired off or formed little groups and, unencumbered by any sort of opprobrium at their behavior, stroked, kissed, and slurped or merely cuddled one another.

Tick placed his arms around me, whether protectively or proprietorially I wasn't sure. All I knew was that I liked it. He kissed the back of my neck and I felt a frisson of desire shoot to my already hard cock, my balls tingling. He ran his hands all over my body, feeling my pecs and my biceps as if he wanted to press the memory to his mind. I felt his cock nudge into my back and I was surprised I didn't mind. In fact, I was pleased he found me sexy.

The air was electric, stirring up emotions as it stirred up the atmosphere, the rain and the thunder competing with the emotions and rampant sexuality sheltering under the rock. We were a seething mass of humanity, intent only on the release of the pent-up respectability of our everyday lives.

Tick whispered in my ear. "I want to taste you."

My censorious brain wanted to shout out its negative reaction to such a thought but my body betrayed me. Tick wrapped his hand around my balls as he wriggled out from behind me and licked his way down my body until he was nearing my pubic area. He skirted my prick in order to tongue my balls, taking each gently into his mouth to suck it lovingly. I stroked his hair as he pleasured me better than I ever had been before. It didn't matter that he was a man with a cock and not a cunt. I didn't care. What the fuck was wrong with me?

Nothing at all. It's just that Tick was so expert at what he did he could have seduced most men. He was what I would have called cute as a button with a man's body, a thick tanned cock and an ass that made your mouth water, although at that stage I didn't know why. Yes, I knew that in some deep recess of my libido I wanted my cock inside him but I didn't know what to do with my mouth. Not yet at any rate.

He ran his thumb over the slick head of my cock while he licked my balls. I thrashed about on the towels blissfully unaware of what the other men were doing or even if they were watching me and Tick. I didn't care. The world consisted of just the two of us even though from time to time I felt other hands caress my body. But it was Tick I wanted. Wanted more than any other person before him.

It was all so unfamiliar to me, I allowed him to take charge, knowing he would lead me safely through the maze. I wondered what the Luke who emerged at the other end would be like.

When he put his tongue to my shaft it was like a bolt of lightning through my body. I couldn't believe a mouth on my prick could be so good. His tongue slicked me up, flicking at the slime oozing from my slit until it was all gone. Then for the best feeling of all as he slid his mouth over my cock like some oral glove, bobbing up and down as he took more and more of my length into his throat. I thought he would gag like all who had gone before him but I was amazed he took me all the way, holding me in his throat as he clutched my shaft by constricting the muscles.

"Holy shit," I panted, holding his head in position. I wanted the feeling to last forever, greedy bastard that I am, even as my mind wondered what Tick would want in return. For a feeling like this I would give him practically anything. I watched as my prick penetrated his mouth and his throat, a feeling of power overwhelming me, a feeling that turned from admiration to, damn it, affection.

"Um, Tick," I grunted, "you may want to…"

I never finished the sentence because Tick doubled his efforts and within minutes I was unable to hold off any longer. I was used to most chicks finishing me off with a hand job but Tick seemed determined to bring me off with his mouth. My cock was so okay with that even if he did spit instead of swallow. I did love to see my spunk on some chicks tongue and I hoped Tick would understand when I asked him to show me his mouth full of spooge before he spat it out on the sand.

Grunting out my request, I thought I saw his nod of acquiescence, hoping I wasn't mistaken. I relaxed into the incredible feeling in my groin, my toes almost curling from the pleasure I was receiving. My hands dug into the towels and the sand beneath as I sought to regain control but it was too late and I shot my wad into his mouth, grunting like an animal as it burst forth. He kept his mouth over my prick until the last spasms emptied my balls and I lay exhausted from the effort even though he had done most of the work.

He pulled off my prick to smile at me and I thought I saw strings of cum drooling from his lips. He opened his mouth and I saw the puddle of my jizz on his tongue but rather than spit, he surprised me by swallowing. My cock was hard as steel at the sight.

I lay panting wondering how I could reciprocate.

"I've never…" I whispered.

"Relax," he said turning his attention back to my balls. It felt so wonderful I almost fell asleep. I would have except I felt my legs being lifted and I knew what his intentions were. I tensed. This was a straight boy's worst nightmare. I'd enjoyed myself so much with Tick, I didn't know how to stop him now. In my mind I didn't think it was a fair swap but it seemed churlish to compare. While the battle raged in my mind, Tick had parted my ass cheeks and planted his tongue at my opening.

I thought they'd have to scrape me off the ceiling of the cave.

"Holy fuck," I screamed.

My girlfriend had managed to wiggle her finger inside my butt, but I had never had a human mouth and tongue sucking, chewing, licking and fucking my hole before. Why didn't anyone tell me about this?

I relaxed even though, at the back of my mind, I knew this was only the preliminary. Still, I didn't want to interrupt this feeling. I knew it would be gone all too soon. Especially when I saw Tick grab a plastic bottle of sun tan lotion and spurt it on his hand. Rubbing it against my butt hole I realized it was too late now although I put up a feeble resistance with, "No, I don't…" But the insertion of his finger, sliding smoothly between the sphincter muscles silenced my objections. He slid in and out of my ass so smoothly, so slickly, it was almost like I'd been born to be fucked.

He managed to find my prostate on his third of fourth plunge and I grunted my approval. That was all he needed to insert another finger and after priming me with those two until my cock drooled, he added a third. The fullness felt so bloody good I almost begged him to fuck me and put me out of my misery.

As he plunged his fingers in and out, his face loomed over mine and I thought I saw love in those deep blue oceans in his eyes. I knew somehow he was seeking my permission before he went any further. I couldn't deny him. I brought his face down to mine, kissing him desperately before releasing him with the request, "Go on, do it."

My ass had been well lubricated by this stage but, nevertheless, he slicked his cock before pressing it against my hole, clenched tight in fright. He pushed and I tensed in expectation. It burned a little but not enough to be uncomfortable. He took his time pushing more and more into me until I felt his balls against my ass. He was buried all the way inside me. I felt full to bursting, not just with Tick's cock but with feelings that confused me and when I looked up into his eyes I thought I saw the same confusion there as well.

He began slowly, pulling out, then pushing back in, increasing the pressure and the speed with each thrust just as a steam engine picks up pace from a cold start. He kissed me at first then began to describe his feelings as he pummeled my ass. I matched him with my verbal expletives, demanding he fuck me harder, faster. I was in this man's thrall. I glanced about to see others indulging much as we were, the group sheltered from the powerful storm outside. It wouldn't always be thus, I knew that.

For now, though, I welcomed Tick's powerful cock inside me, begging him to give it to me hard. I knew I meant more than just his cock. I wanted him to give me so much more and I wondered if he could possibly ever want the same.

"I can't hold on much longer," he gasped. "Your ass is so good, I just gotta come."

"Fill my ass with your spunk," I said. "I want to feel you inside me. Your cock in my ass is the best feeling ever."

"I could fuck you all night, Luke."

"I love the feel of your cock, Tick," I replied.

There was so much more I wanted to say but Tick moaned loudly and I felt his spunk shoot into my bowels and the moment passed. He collapsed on top of me and I could feel his heart beating wildly in his chest. I ran my fingers down his back and into his ass crack until I found his moist hole.

"You'll have to wait a while for your turn, Luke," he said breathlessly. "I'm buggered."

He rolled off me before kissing me, scooping me up in his arms.

He seemed unsure now. "You do want a turn, don't you?" he asked.

"Hell, yeah," I said throwing my arms around him wondering how I could keep this amazing man for a little while longer. "I have a lot to learn. I need a good teacher."

Tick leaned back against my chest. "I'm not doing anything. I could teach you."

"You won't get bored?"

"I don't think I could ever get bored with you," he said.

I hugged him tighter, wondering if it was too soon to suggest he come to the city so we could both go to the same university the following year.

The New Dad's Club

"I told you they'd treat you as their personal drudge and babysitter," Karl said as I turned down his invitation to the slave auction that Sunday afternoon.

"Shit," I moaned. I'd had visions of making a bid or two on Lincoln who was so hot that just his bare feet touching the pavement was enough to melt concrete. He was between boyfriends and I was just perfect for what he needed – although he didn't know that as yet.

"I bet they dump her on you every weekend while they go out with their friends but you don't get invited to any of the special events like birthdays or first baby steps."

"She hasn't had any of those yet," I replied, secretly admitting to myself that he was right. Chloe's two mothers never invited me to those special occasions when they had all their female friends over. Perhaps I should have a party one weekend to show off the result of jerking my sprog into a plastic cup.

Chloe was the sweetest little girl. She had blonde hair and blue eyes, just like me, as opposed to her mother's darker hair and eyes. It was no great hardship babysitting her while her mums got a bit of rest and recreation. It was just galling that I was always called on for the weekends when I needed to be out finding a boyfriend. Not to put too fine a point on it, I was getting on in gay years and the first flush of youth was already down the toilet and around the U-bend. If I didn't find a boyfriend soon there was no hope for me and I'd have to advertise myself on Silver Daddies just to get laid. Okay, I'm a bit of a drama queen, but Karl and I were the only two in our gang of friends who didn't have partners. That over half of them were either clandestinely or overtly cheating on their partners was beside the point. I know love can get stale after you've been together for more than six weeks and the grass is always greener on the other side.

Now opportunity was sliding through my fingers in much the same way Chloe's diapers did because the smell made me barf. Chloe's mums, Desiree and Georgia, had dropped off their daughter as well as a bag full of dirty nappies for me to wash because I had a machine in my building and they would have had to go to the Laundromat. Can anyone say, Lazy Lesbians?

I know they didn't earn much by way of wages what with businesses seeing slave labor when they looked at women, but it's not as if I had a lot of money either. I helped out as best I could but as I listened to Karl rabbit on about his adventures I realized how much disruption a kid can cause, especially when she wasn't even officially mine. My name didn't appear on the birth certificate alongside her two mums, which I thought was wrong. I wanted Chloe to know who her donor dad was even if that made me sound like a kebab.

"Don't say I didn't warn you," Karl repeated.

But then I looked at Chloe and my innards turned to mush and I became just like all those other soppy bastards with kids. Don't knock it till you try it.

"As long as you have…that…" Karl was still having difficulty getting his lips around my daughter's name, unlike his complete lack of difficulty getting his lips, tongue and throat around any stranger's dick, so he merely called her 'that' and pointed.

"Her name is Chloe," I said. "Say it after me, Klo-ee. Klo-ee."

He batted me across the back of the head in jest. "As long as you have her who shall not be named, you'll have no chance in hell of getting yourself a boyfriend. No one wants an unmarried dad as a boyfriend. Especially if you draw the short straw as babysitter every weekend."

I would have to discuss this with Chloe's mums. It was getting to be a bit of an inconvenience. Looking on the bright side: they did trust me enough to leave their daughter with me. On top of that…

Chloe let out one of her ear-piercing wails.

"On that note, time for Uncle Karl to say his goodbyes. That's the alarm that signals breaking out the air freshener and as I have an ultra-sensitive nose, I think I should make my departure."

I air kissed Karl before picking Chloe out of her basinet, wrinkling my nose at that all-too-familiar odor. I'd become quite adept at the old diaper routine and had her changed and snug in a matter of minutes unlike my first feeble efforts which had taken forever because I'd taken so long to overcome my gag reflex, something I'd had no trouble with up until that experience.

Chloe was restless, but I knew the perfect solution. She loved it when I took her for a walk so, as I needed to head around to the post office to pick up mail the postman had declared too large to fit in my apartment letterbox, this was the perfect opportunity for us to venture forth into the fresh air. I dressed her in her outdoor gear including the floppy hat to protect her head and face from the sun and lowered her into the baby harness which I wore on my back with her little head against my shoulder blades.

She gurgled happily as we left the apartment. She was anticipating the elevator and her little arms waved about as the mechanical voice counted off the floors as we descended and the final ping as we reached the ground floor sent her off into positive burbles of delight which meant she was probably drooling all over the back of my shirt.

It was a warm, sunny day as I dawdled down the street toward the main intersection which would take me into the shopping center. On the corner was a park with the ubiquitous Lest We Forget memorial to the men and women who had died fighting various wars since the Great War of 1914-1918. It was strewn with rotting wreaths of flowers left over from some memorial long forgotten except by those whose loved ones had perished. Council workers were unceremoniously feeding them into a shredder reducing the detritus to compost. It would be spread much later on the park's beds of roses and smaller flowering plants such as pansies and peonies, as well as around the native bushes that attracted insects and birds.

I found a convenient seat off one of the less used paths and unstrapped Chloe so she could watch in her immature way. She reached out for everything that moved, unafraid of passing mutts who went to sniff the little alien life form, or butterflies that hovered as if unsure whether she was animal, vegetable or mineral but intelligent enough to stay out of her sticky slobbery reach.

These moments made up for all those occasions when I thought I was being shamelessly abused, although deep down I was pleased Desiree and Georgia didn't exclude me from Chloe's upbringing even if I was mainly just a drudge. It made up for all those nights I missed seeing my friends at the bars or the clubs. On those social occasions I would inevitably spend too much money, go home alone pissed off my face or, even worse, go home pissed and drug fucked with some man or men I wouldn't recognize the next morning. That's if the coupling went that long. Often I found myself in a frighteningly unfamiliar street in the early hours of the morning attempting to hail a non-existent cab hoping I had enough money in my wallet to get me safely home.

Sometimes, when my wallet and my rainy day money had been insufficient to cover the expense of a ride home, I paid with my mouth or my ass. I wasn't proud of the levels to which I'd stooped but until Mister Right came along a fuck is a fuck is a fuck as Gertrude Stein would have said if she'd been a gay man. Ditto for a suck.

I'd been searching for love in all the wrong places. Everywhere, actually. They'd all turned out disastrously: from the pretentious tie salesman who worked for an upmarket men's boutique and liked to…

"What a cute baby," a voice shrieked, interrupting my waking mind dreams.

Opening one eye I found a young woman's face so close to my own I could smell the flavor of the gum with which she was blowing a giant sticky bubble to tease Chloe.

"What's her name?"

"Chloe," I answered moving the child away from the sticky mass which would infuriate Desiree if it got in Chloe's hair.

"Aw, that's soooo cute," said the young woman's female friend.

They cooed and chattered seemingly reluctant to leave.

"Is she yours?" the more brazen girl asked.

"Yes," I answered brusquely, hoping they would go away and leave me and Chloe in peace.

"Ooh, she's got your eyes," the other gushed.

Yes, she had. Everyone said so. I didn't need two flirtatious young women telling me so.

"See," the gum chewer said, turning to her friend, "I told you he wasn't gay, Tina."

Shit, they really were flirting. Time to let them know I was penile inclined.

"As a matter of fact, Tina's right, I am gay."

"See, I told ya," Tina gloated.

Gum Girl withdrew quickly, muttering, "Poor little kid."

They both wandered away cursing me for their disappointment. When I looked around to see if anyone had witnessed our conversation, I noticed a good-looking guy around my age seated farther along the brick-paved path staring at me. He was nursing a child who was sucking and drooling some sort of brightly colored sweet all over its face. I had no way of telling if the child was a boy or a girl.

He smiled, nodding his head toward the two young women as they exited the park. "Slags," he said. "You were right to turn them down."

The women had ignored him with, I thought, a sort of contempt as if they knew him as they'd passed. There was obviously a history there. He was far enough away that he couldn't have heard me tell them I was gay for which I was grateful as the area was solidly working class and not exactly gay friendly, at least not this part of the suburb.

He gathered up his child and wandered over to where I was seated, his eyes enquiring whether I would be amenable to his sitting with me.

"Please," I said, moving to give him space.

"Neil," he said, proffering me his hand. "This is Jenny."

I introduced myself and Chloe.

"This your first?" he asked.

"Uh huh."

"You probably haven't stumbled across the secret then," he smiled. "Or maybe you have as you're sitting here in the park like this."

"Just on my way to the shops," I said. "Chloe likes the colors and the plants so I thought I'd take a short break. I didn't know babies could be so heavy."

"That's not all they are," he laughed.

"Oh?"

"Chick magnets, mate. That's what babies are."

"What do you mean?"

"Those girls who were chatting you up."

"What about them?"

"Dick mad," he said. "They've propositioned just about every new dad in the park. If a man's got a young baby with him, they're drawn to the guy like flies to shit. They're not the only ones. Lots of chicks are."

I was amused at his casual sexism although Chloe's mums would have had his balls for ear-rings. "You speak from experience?"

"Of course. Had those two slags the first week after I joined the New Dad's Club."

"The New Dad's Club? What's that?"

"Just a group of us guys who bring our kids to the park on a set day each week in order to give our wives a break."

"You all know one another?"

"We didn't to begin with but a couple of us kept bumping into each other, discovered we were...ah... likeminded, and we sort of formed this unofficial group and it took off from there."

"Likeminded?"

"Yeah," he whispered conspiratorially, "we discovered we like pussy and not just our wife's. We also discovered that carrying a baby attracts all kinds of women who ooh and ahh over the kid and quite often are prepared to give us doting dads a bit of a free ride. That's why we banded together."

If only it worked on gay men. Maybe it does, but I was unlikely to find out in this suburban park. I'd need to visit the gay area to test the waters.

"You all get pussy on the side?" I asked.

He nodded. "Except Greg. His missus died in childbirth. A real tragedy. He hasn't got over it yet."

"Shit, that's awful."

"Can we count you in? Your Chloe will be a real chick puller. I think having a new face in the group will rekindle some of the interest that's been missing lately."

"Um…"

"No pressure, mate. You can take it at your own speed. In case you're worried, we have a hands-off policy toward each other's wives."

"Let me think it over." I settled Chloe back in her harness and stood up to continue our journey.

"You won't regret it. A good-looking guy like you will be sinking his dick in stray pussy in no time flat."

I felt like telling him it wasn't going to happen and that his attitude was not a ringing endorsement of the New Dad's Club charter but I held my tongue. I didn't need to make enemies of the local straight brigade.

As I made my way toward the main thoroughfare into the shopping center, Neil called after me, "The club has other benefits as well. We share babysitting duty for one. Why don't you drop by…?" He reeled off the day and time the men met. Okay, Neil was a looker and seemed to have a body that was hard as the pavement beneath my feet but there seemed little chance that he'd point his dick in my direction.

I soon forgot our meeting as I concentrated on the tasks at hand and it wasn't until I was walking back to my apartment, once again cutting through the park, seeing Neil and another man chatting amiably that I made a decision. I would join the group. It was lonely sitting at home looking after Chloe while her mums were away, so provided the conversation was not too caveman-like I'd be okay. It might also help Chloe to socialize, if there was such a thing as her age, with locals. And…it was the biggest plus of all…if the guy talking to Neil was a member then I was definitely a contender. I was hoping the new man was the club president and that the entry requirement was to suck his dick.

Yum! Sure, Neil was a stud and I'd definitely go there for a one or two-off, but the other guy was marriage material. Pity he was holding a baby about the same age as Chloe. That meant a wife or life partner hovering in the background.

Neil leaned over to whisper in his mate's ear as they watched me approach. When I drew parallel it seemed impolite not to stop.

"This is the guy I was telling you about," Neil said but I was unsure if he was talking to me or the stranger. "Jason, Greg."

I took the strong, masculine hand that was offered, liking the warmth of the grip: not too strong, not too limp – just right.

This was the guy whose wife had died. I slapped my brain for immediately tagging him available. Tacky. I couldn't help myself. He was adorable; everything I looked for in a man. Hot, hairy, hung – if the bulge in his shorts was to be believed – and his smile was like honey. His eyes crinkled in the corners when he smiled. I gazed into his eyes to see if there was any sort of spark but there was none.

Somewhat embarrassed, I realized I still had hold of his hand. I let go, attempting to cover my gaucherie by a lie, "I thought I might know you. You looked familiar from a distance, but now I see you up close…" I shook my head.

He smiled. "I've got one of those generic faces that reminds people of someone they know."

Anything but generic, I thought, but did not say out loud.

Neil said it for me. "Greg is our looker. Attracts women like the sole of a shoe attracts chewing gum. We get to reap the benefits."

"Why don't you join us for a coffee?" Greg asked. "There's a child friendly café just across the road."

No way was I going to turn down an invitation from this man. Besides, I was in no hurry. All I had planned was a return to an empty apartment. Chloe was sleeping soundly so I could afford a little 'me' time.

The café was fairly deserted this time of the morning, too early for the lunch crowd, so we were able to spread out. Tony, the elderly proprietor, knew the guys and welcomed us effusively, including me in his friendly banter. I was introduced as the newest member of the club and as a welcome all my drinks were free.

"This is a friendly place," I said as I relaxed for the first time that day. The café was simply called Tony's Place, essentially a storefront with folding doors to allow tables and chairs to spill out onto the street in hot weather. The menu was mainly easily prepared snacks with a smattering of mains for those who wanted simple Italian cooking.

"Tony's lived in the area since he migrated here in the early 1950s," Greg told me. "He found there were already too many Italian barbers when he arrived so he opened his café to serve them food from home. The only spaghetti available locally in those days came in tins. Plus he knew how to brew Italian-style coffee."

"Many of the old people who settled in the area have gone now," Tony said as he handed us our coffees. I took a sip and it was wonderful. I'd be back here with or without the club. Neil pulled out a chair and nodded that Tony should join us.

"When the Italians settled in the area, they set up market gardens because the land was cheap and they couldn't find the fresh ingredients they used in the old country. Gradually, the Italian influence spread into the wider community until today it's the most prevalent cuisine in the country."

Tony produced a number of mismatched glasses and a bottle of home-made wine. Sure it tasted as if he merely scraped the gravel off the road outside and melted it down before sealing it in a bottle, but it had quite a kick to it and I was pleasantly mellow as the morning progressed. Chloe woke up and I fed her the bottle I always carried with me for such occasions, Tony kindly heating it slightly in his miniature kitchen.

As people began to arrive for the lunch rush, I realized we'd been sitting talking for two hours and I had a buzz on. Neil had flown the coop a while before but I'd been having such a great time with Greg I hadn't once looked at my watch. He was a genuinely nice guy and we had a number of interests in common including our taste in Jason Statham adventure movies. I suspect, however, his appreciation had less to do with how hot the actor and his ripped body were, than mine did.

I got the distinct impression Greg had less of a social life than me. He lived for his little boy, Kees, working from home on web design, with little time off for meeting people. I gathered the New Dad's Club was the sum total of the socializing he managed. He seemed to have little by way of support at home but I felt at that early stage it was not my place to pry. By the time we parted, I was convinced I had met the man I wanted to spend the remainder of my life with.

Fortunately, the fresh air on the walk back to my apartment slapped the reality of the situation into my head. What the hell was I thinking joining a group of bad-ass straight men who used their babies to lure women for sex? I really would have to think this over before next week when I'd promised I'd turn up for seconds.

Somewhere during those seven days my conscience went on vacation and my common sense did a runner. I turned up, Chloe in tow, to meet a few of the rotating members. They were a nondescript gaggle of horny straight men whose conversation I listened to rather than participated in, especially when it came to sports in which I had no interest, and women's sexual statistics in which I had even less. A couple of the men were downright gross in their sexual appetites for the opposite sex and Neanderthal in their attitudes. I mainly sat and listened, making up just enough about 'my wife Georgia' to keep them unsuspicious while they bantered about their conquests.

They were correct in one respect: the number of women who descended on the park in groups or solo while the men lazed on the seats with their babies. A constant stream of women patted and petted, and surreptitiously groped when they thought no one was looking. Greg deflected any familiarity as did I after the first couple of attempts took me by surprise. The other men took it as their due, swapping phone numbers and times they were available.

Only a small group adjourned to Tony's: Neil, Greg, Pat and myself usually. Neil and Pat spoke about their conquests while I was ribbed about my reluctance to join in the smorgasbord of sexual offerings. It was unspoken, but Greg was off limits when it came to good-natured ribbing about extramarital relationships. I enjoyed my mornings with 'the boys' – especially one of them. I knew I should stop my attendance because it would lead only to heartache – or worse. I simply couldn't help myself.

"You intend to do what?" Karl practically shouted. I'd made the mistake of telling him all about the New Dad's Club. I must have made it sound far too interesting because he threatened to borrow a baby and come along himself just to check out the dads. I managed to persuade him it wasn't a good idea. But when I told him I was falling for Greg, he blustered. "Your problem is you've let those lesbians impose for too long. Next weekend you are definitely taking time out to get laid in order to banish this ridiculous idea of a hook-up with a straight man out of your head."

"Uh," he said as I went to protest. "It will do you no good. I will be here next Saturday night ready to help get you all shagged out. If, by some strange quirk of fate, you are still alone and unfucked at the end of the night, I will drag you home and fuck you myself." He sighed theatrically. "Ah, the things I do for my friends."

"What if I have Chloe with me?"

"I swear, Jason, if you have that baby with you when I arrive, I will personally take her back to her lesbian mothers and jam her back up her mother's—"

"I guess it wouldn't hurt to take one weekend off."

Desiree and Georgia were understanding about my needs although they attempted to spread guilt like manure all over the seedlings of my plans. In the event, Karl didn't have to follow through with his threat of bedding me because I found a perfectly respectable man with a very respectable job – he was an accountant – and he had a very acceptable penis which he used acceptably well. In the morning I accepted his cell phone number and he accepted mine. By lunchtime, I'd all but forgotten him.

By evening I couldn't recall his name until my mobile phone rang and his name appeared. It took me a few seconds to wonder who the hell this Nathan was and how he'd wormed his way onto the friends' list on my phone. It wasn't until he responded to my very tentative 'Jason speaking' with "I want to thank you again for last night. It was wonderful," that I recognized his name.

We chatted a while longer but I guess he heard the disinterest in my voice because rather than ask for another date which I suspected was the purpose of his call, he merely reiterated, "Thanks again for a wonderful evening. Call me if you want to do it again some time."

I didn't want to encourage him, so ended with the feeble, "Sure. Will do."

It wasn't his fault, Mr. whatever his name is. It was simply that I couldn't get Greg out of my mind. Even fucking someone else, it was Greg's name I wanted to call out in the throes of passion. Karl was right, I'm a fool. Still, I intended going ahead with my plan anyway. Karl obviously had other ideas.

I went to the park with Chloe for the usual New Dad's Club 'meeting.' Before handing over their daughter, the two mums, Desiree in particular, let it be known that my intransigence in wanting a weekend off had seriously inconvenienced them. "We don't get much time just to be together, you know. Surely a weekend and a day during the week is not too much to ask from Chloe's father?"

That pissed me off and I retaliated childishly. "So, I'm Chloe's father now? Not what it says on the birth certificate."

Georgia was quite cavalier about my sexual needs. "Why don't you settle down with someone? You gay guys are so promiscuous."

"If I had the chance to meet someone, I just might settle down, but as I am forced to sit at home every Friday and Saturday night, the two most important gay men's nights of the week, it's highly unlikely."

We parted badly, although not badly enough that Georgia and Desiree took Chloe with them. I was grateful for that and thought that, perhaps, I'd been a little petulant. Too late now. Strapping Chloe into her harness, I headed out to meet the guys, nervous at what I was about to do. There were five of us that day; the weather being overcast and slightly cool had kept other dads, as well as many of the women who circled the park like human ravens, away. At least Neil was there. Ordinarily, he's loads to fun to talk to but that day he was skittish and jittery, barely able to sit still for more than a few seconds. He must have noticed me watching his odd behavior.

"Blue balls, mate. I gotta get laid. Wife's got that post-partum depression shit. I can't handle it."

"She may need help, Neil. Has she seen someone?"

"Yeah, I sent her back home to her folks for a week or two."

"That's not what I meant."

It wasn't really my place to lecture Neil on his wife's mental health but I was in a 'mood' as well. Everyone around me seemed to be: Karl telling me how to live my life, just as I was interfering with Neil's marriage, just as Chloe's mums were nagging at me for inconveniencing them, just as...

My life was as fucked as anyone's. Suddenly my head felt like it needed to explode just so I could get some sanity back into my life. What the hell was I doing lusting after a straight man whose wife had died but a few months previously? What was I doing mixing with a mob of sexist assholes who used their babies as a lure to fuck women? What was I doing using my own daughter to mix socially with these bastards?

Somewhere in the past few months I'd obviously taken a wrong turn. It was time to get back to the crossroads and try a different path. That's precisely what I would have done if a number of things hadn't occurred. First, Neil sat up on the park bench, arranging his baby daughter, Jenny, on his lap as you would a display model and whispered out of the side of his mouth. "If she stops to talk, make an excuse and piss off."

"Who?"

I didn't need an answer because right then a voice cooed, "Oh my, aren't they the sweetest little babies."

I looked up into the eyes of a very attractive young woman with so much blonde hair it must have taken the entire peroxide supplies of a Third World nation. She was making those eyes that adults are prone to make around babies and didn't know whether to pounce on Chloe or Jenny. Neil elbowed me hard, almost pushing me off the seat. I regained my balance and with my brightest smile, made some excuse which sounded feeble even to me, and stood to leave. Neil and the blonde scarcely acknowledged my departure; they were making eyes at each other, Jenny all but ignored.

It was too much. I stormed off unnoticed by anyone and headed to Tony's Café. I was in need of one of his comfort coffees and an Italian cake.

Tony was wiping down the tables as I entered his small establishment. "On your own today?"

"The others may be along later," I lied. I sat at a table watching the park while Tony fussed getting my order. Neil and his blonde conquest seemed deep in conversation, their heads bowed, almost touching. From a distance it looked as if they were admiring Jenny. I felt a sudden sadness for Neil's wife.

"Oh, here you are."

The voice startled me from my reverie. I had been so engrossed in the behavior of the denizens of the park I had not noticed his approach. My heart thumped wildly, my pulse raced, my face flushed. I couldn't believe I allowed myself to get this way over Greg.

"What are you doing here?" I asked.

"I couldn't stand the idea of the park today. All that testosterone exhausts me sometimes."

I smiled. "Me, too."

I pulled a chair out for him as his arms were full with Kees who was wriggling like an eel.

"Thanks." He exhaled deeply as he sat.

"Bad day?" I enquired.

"Bad week."

"Me, too."

"Can't sleep."

"Kees disrupting your dreams?"

"Definitely." He paused as if contemplating revealing a secret. "But it's more than that."

"Anything you care to talk about?"

"I wish I could."

I shrugged. "There's always a friendly shoulder available at my number."

He looked me in the eye. "Just how friendly, I wonder?"

"What on earth—"

What did he mean? Had he twigged to my true sexuality? I'd be left to wonder a while longer because Neil chose that moment to crash our small party.

"Same as usual, Tony," he called as he beamed at Greg and I. "No more blue balls for me."

"You got her number?" I asked.

"Piece of piss," he announced with pride. "Once she saw Jenny, it was all over."

Greg asked the question that I'd bitten off before I could ask it. It did not pay to be too moral around Neil. "Tell me, doesn't she mind that you have a wife?"

Neil didn't seem to notice the tone of disapproval in Greg's voice. "Nah, she's not after anything serious. Just a good fuck every now and then. I've shown her my virility bona fides with Jenny, plus she knows I'm unavailable except for pleasure. No strings attached. Suits us both. We're going out on Friday night, provided I can get a babysitter."

"Oh, no you don't. I'm not sleeping these days. I don't need another one to look after even for a few hours. Find someone else."

"You know your problem, Greg? You need to get laid." Neil was a brave man venturing into territory we'd all accepted as too personal. "Sure, you loved your wife but it's over. You can keep the memory alive in here." Neil tapped his heart. "And here." His head. "But it won't help you out here, mate." He went to tap Greg's crotch but withdrew his hand when Greg looked daggers at him.

To prevent an argument, I changed the subject. "Friday night, eh? Doesn't do your blue balls much good at the moment."

"Damn, Jason. You think I need a reminder?" Neil adjusted his trousers. "I'm so fuckin' horny I'd settle for a blow job from one of you."

Greg almost spat his coffee across the café and the look of horror on his face gave me an attack of the giggles. Neil soon joined in. Greg was as red as a rash on a baby's bottom.

"It was just as expression, mate," Neil said. "Just a joke."

Greg pouted. "Sometimes I can't tell with you."

The atmosphere between the three of us was suddenly strained. This was not helping me with my plan. Just when I thought the situation couldn't get any stickier, I heard a voice that made me want to crawl under the table.

"Jason, I've been trying to call you. Why the fuck don't you answer your phone?"

I groaned inwardly. Neil and Greg both looked up to examine the creature who had interrupted our funk.

Karl stood with his hand dramatically on his hip as if posing for some swishy gay calendar. I knew he was doing it deliberately to provoke me, or one of my companions, because Karl never stood like this any other time.

"Oooh," he minced. "Who are these two attractive men you're with? You are a sly dog. I'm Karl, Jason's best friend." He held out his hand as if he expected the two men to kiss it rather than shake it. They did neither, merely smiling at him in a bemused manner.

I had no choice. "Neil, Greg, this is a friend of mine, Karl."

Much as I wanted to at that moment, I wasn't about to disown him.

Karl didn't know when to keep his mouth shut. "You're the two guys Jason is always talking about. Especially you, Greg." Karl made a great show of occupying the vacant seat.

Greg looked at me with a quizzical look.

"You're the two guys from that New Daddy's Group he's always mentioning." Karl batted his eyelids, crossed his legs, licked his lips, then cooed, "I'm looking for a daddy and either one of you would suit me just fine."

Greg obviously hadn't forgiven Neil's joke from earlier because he said, "There you go, Neil. You were moaning about blue balls earlier. I'm sure Karl could take care of them for you."

"Blue balls are my specialty," Karl boasted.

The café was beginning to fill up with lunch-time patrons and three of us were squirming, wondering in which direction the conversation would head next. Karl rapped me on the arm. "Have you asked them yet?"

"Asked them what?"

Karl huffed as if I was totally useless. "I thought you were going to invite them back to your apartment today for lunch. I brought all the groceries like you asked."

I'd asked no such thing. And it was only Greg I'd intended inviting.

"Where do you live exactly?" Neil asked.

Karl didn't give me a chance to answer.

"Three blocks in that direction," he swished, using a cake fork to point, almost taking out another patron's eye. "You must come, I'm preparing the most amazing lunch."

"I had no idea you lived around here," Greg said. "We all come from farther afield."

"So no one we run into will know us," Neil admitted sheepishly. "I can see now why you were more circumspect. A man shouldn't shit in his own backyard."

Karl stood, hassling us to follow him. "I presume you hot guys both have your cars with you. Okay, Greg, you can take Jason and I'll go with Neil here." So saying he wrapped his arm around Neil and dragged him from the café, barely giving his captive time to grab his baby daughter. "See you back at your place, Jason."

"You really don't have to come back," I said to Greg as I paid the bill. "Karl made up all that shit about making lunch."

"No, I'd love to come back. This casts a whole different light on your character."

I wasn't sure if that was a good or a bad thing.

Greg's car was around the corner in a side street. I decided it was best to get it out in the open now, before I got into Greg's car.

"What was that crack earlier about wondering how friendly I was?"

Greg was silent for a while. "I haven't been entirely honest with you."

What could I say? I hadn't been entirely honest with him either.

"Right."

"There's a very good reason why I can't sleep. Why I've been crabby for a couple of weeks now. Impossible to be with."

"Sounds like the same symptoms I've got," I said.

Greg laughed. "Yeah, well it won't be from the same cause, I guarantee it."

"I know about your wife, Greg. And I'm sorry."

"She wasn't my wife."

"In this day and age it doesn't matter if you're married. I don't hold with all that moral shit."

"No, you don't understand."

We were at his car. He beeped the locking system and he strapped Kees into the child restraint. "You'll have to nurse Chloe until we get back to your place. I'm a very careful driver."

"I trust you," I said.

Once we were all settled in the car, Greg drove off slowly. We didn't talk much as I was guiding him to my apartment and that took all our concentration. My space in the building car park was near the lifts and we rode up in silence, or as much like silence when you have two babies gurgling contentedly.

I unlocked the door to my apartment and ushered in Greg and Kees. Greg looked like an animal caught in headlights but a little push and he was inside. I don't know why he was so nervous. I put Chloe in her playpen and suggested Greg put Kees in with her. They were roughly the same age and I expected they'd get along fine. In fact, they'd probably both be asleep in next to no time.

Once we'd ensured Chloe and Kees were settled, I turned to Greg. "So tell me what I don't understand."

Greg took a deep breath and closed the brief space between the two of us, planting his lips on mine before I'd even had a chance to open my mouth in surprise. His lips were sweet; they tasted of coffee and the raspberry and chocolate muffin he ate at Tony's. I got my mouth open and welcomed his invasion, while wrapping my arms around his broad, muscular back. I guess he wasn't expecting me to kiss him back because I noticed his eyes flicker open in surprise.

When we had to break for breath, I asked, "Is that what was keeping you awake lately?"

"Uh huh."

"Me, too."

"So, Chloe?"

"Sperm donor."

Greg laughed raucously. "I thought you were so straight, talking about your wife and all that."

"What about you and your dead wife?"

"That much was true."

Me and my big mouth.

"Well, not my wife. My best female friend. I could never marry her. Could never do the dirty with her. She wanted a baby so desperately, so I helped her out.

Jerking off into a plastic cup. The birth was difficult and…" he paused to get his emotions in check.

I finished the sentence for him. "She didn't make it?"

"Her dying wish was that I bring up Kees. It's been hard."

"No social life?"

"None at all. No one wants a gay guy with a baby."

I flirted. "I wouldn't be so sure of that."

"What about you?"

"Donor to two women I know. They're a couple. I look after Chloe a couple of times a week to give them a break."

"Must cruel your social life a bit as well."

"Yeah."

"Is that why you joined New Dad's Club?"

"That was an accident. Neil mistook me for a straight dad and it was pleasant company in the beginning although it stuck in my craw the way he and some of the others treated women. Then…"

"What?"

"I guess it doesn't matter if I tell you now. I started to fall for you."

"You gay or bi or just curious?"

"Definitely gay. Out and proud," I admitted.

"Me, too."

"Then why—"

"I hope you don't decide the kiss was not a good idea when I tell you."

I ran my finger across my lips which were still tingling. "I'll never think that."

"Someone told me about this group of guys who tended to congregate in the park and some of them were really hot and didn't mind who they stuck their dick in."

"Neil, for example?" I asked.

Greg nodded.

"I guess we shouldn't expect Karl to turn up any time soon?"

"That would be a very safe bet."

"Mmm, in that case it gives us more time to get to know each other a whole lot better."

Greg looked uncomfortable. "I'm not a slut."

"I didn't think you were."

"I'm sort of looking for something a bit longer-term than a one-night stand."

"I hear you."

"The only reason I kept going back was I couldn't stop thinking of you…"

"I couldn't stop thinking about you…"

"I thought you were straight"

"I thought you were straight."

We stumbled back and forth over each other's sentences until we both collapsed in laughter. I stared at this beautiful man whom I'd met scant months ago. Was it too soon to start falling in love?

"I know what you're thinking," he said as he ran his hand down the side of my face.

"Yeah?"

"You're wondering if it's too soon. Well, so am I."

"I like you a lot, Greg."

"I like you a lot, Jason. But I've got a baby. Not one that can be returned at the end of the day. He's for keeps, with all his attendant problems."

"Did I mention I love kids?"

"Did I mention I could get very used to having you around on a more permanent basis?"

We went into a clinch that would have seared the paint off the wall if Kees hadn't begun to wail.

"I guess someone needs their diaper changed," Greg sighed.

"I'll help you. I'm an expert at it."

It took no time at all to change the wriggling little boy.

"He has your eyes. He'll be a handsome little bugger when he grows up. Just like his daddy."

I picked Kees up and held him to face me. He reached out for my nose and gave it a good tug with his little hands.

"Kees, I want to get your permission before I do anything. You think maybe I could ask your daddy out on a date?"

He made gurgling sounds, blowing spit bubbles between his lips.

"I'll take that as a yes." I kissed him on the forehead. I turned to Greg. "How about it?"

"I can't think of anything I'd like better."

Greg folded his arms around me and Kees. I didn't think either of us would be returning to the New Dad's Club. We'd found what we'd been looking for.

Lydian

About the Author

Barry Lowe writes about love and sex so he won't forget how to do it. When he's not scribbling his adventures for the Sydney gay weekly *SX*, or out doing field research, he's writing about love's wonderful variations for a series of smut eBooks, novels and anthologies for Lydian Press.

Go to www.barrylowe.info

ANTHOLOGIES By Barry Lowe

BUSTING BILLY'S BUTT - eBook & Print

Four On The Floor
Jolly Rogering
The Devil His Due
Never Take Candy from Strangers
Done Like A Dinner
In The Family Way
Right Up His Alley
Group Therapy

THE MAJOR AND THE MINERS - eBook & Print

A Serpent in Paradise
Desperate Remedies
Joshua's Story
Emerald City
Danny's Revenge
Future Tense

ROMANCING THE BONE - eBook and Print

Carbon Dating
Let the Games Begin
Taking the Bait
Party Whip
Team Player
Davy Jones' Locker
Here's to You, Mr Robinson
Gay Dungeon for the Straight Boy
OMG! Santa's Got a Six-Pack
Vlad the Impaler
Meta-Analysis of the Effects of Love on Tofu

LIKE FATHER LIKE SON - eBook and Print

Man of the Hour
Like Father Like Son
Sonny & Shared
Sonny Side Up
Eclipse Of The Son
Son & Games
Where The Sun Don't Shine
The Sun Shines Out Of His Ass
Have Son Will Travel

BABY, I'M NOT A MONSTER - eBook and Print

The Vampire's Guide to Dental Hygiene
Stupid Cupid
Gadigal
Pride & Joy
Seeing Things
My Dad's a Vampire
Guys & Trolls

ROUGH & READY - eBook and Print

Stocks & Shared
Scarface
Ceps: Mad about Muscle
The Plumbers' Mate*
Climbing Up the Wall
Little Red Rides da Hood
The Dex Factor
Jailhouse Cock
The Skinhead Upstairs

OMG! NOT ANOTHER GAY EROTICA ANTHOLOGY?

OMG! My Dad's a Stripper!

OMG! The College Jock's a Nudist!

OMG! Put Some Clothes On!

OMG! My Uncle's a Fairy!

OMG! Satan Wants a Blow Job!

OMG! My Dad's Got Tits!

OMG! Santa's Got a Six-pack!

YOUR BOYFRIEND IS HOT - eBook and Print

From Here to Fraternity

Stripping His Assets

Indecent Exposure

Middle Man for Madame Blavatsky

A Cook's Tour

Topping the Pizza Delivery Boy

THE BOY IS A BOTTOM - eBook and Print

Marine Biology

Marine Animals

Attack of the Ass Bandits

The Arab Downstairs

Clockwork Derriere

Creaming the Party Dip

Top of the World

Route 666: Signal Driver

The Butler Did Him

Fifty Shades of Fey

Spinning the Bottom

For all Barry's titles please visit his page at:
lydianpress.com

Lydian Press is dedicated to bringing you the finest GLBTQ erotic literature on the web.

Visit us on the web at:
http://lydianpress.com

www.ingramcontent.com/pod-product-compliance
Lightning Source LLC
Chambersburg PA
CBHW051045050726
47592CB00002B/399